KATHERINE PATERSON

JIP
His Story

SCHOLASTIC INC.

New York Toronto London Auckland Sydney
Mexico City New Delhi Hong Kong

ISBN 0-439-05388-9

Copyright © 1996 by Minna Murra, Inc.
All rights reserved.
Published by Scholastic Inc., 555 Broadway, New York, NY 10012,
by arrangement with Puffin Books, a division of Penguin Putnam Inc.
SCHOLASTIC and associated logos are trademarks and/or registered
trademarks of Scholastic Inc.

12 11 10 9 8 7 6 5 4 3 2 1   8 9/9 0 1 2 3/0

Printed in the U.S.A.   40

First Scholastic printing, November 1998

for those who
have made this gypsy
feel at home
in Vermont,
especially
Nancy Graff and Grace Greene

Acknowledgments

Particular thanks must go to Nancy Graff for reading this book in manuscript and making several pages' worth of helpful suggestions, though any errors of fact that remain are, of course, my own. Thanks, too, to Larry Gordon, who kindly located the music for the hymn "All Is Well" from his library of early American music, to Lindsay Graff, my moose consultant, and to Alison Hall for sharing her experience with sheep. I am also grateful to the staffs of the Vermont Historical Society and the Vermont State Library, and, especially, to Marjorie Strong of the Aldrich Library in Barre, Vermont.

Although the events of this story are fictional, the character of Put Nelson is based on an actual nineteenth–century Vermonter, Putnam Proctor Wilson, who lived in a cage on the town poor farm in Hartford. According to the town history, when he was rational, Putnam Wilson loved to sing to children and would sing the same song over and over as often as requested. I want to thank Mary Sorum and Dr. Christopher Meyers for their help as I tried to understand in modern medical terms the condition Putnam Wilson's contemporaries regarded as lunacy.

As my pile of books grows ever higher, so does my debt of gratitude to John Paterson and Virginia Buckley. Once again, thank you both.

Contents

My life began the afternoon of June 7, 1847, when I tumbled off the back of a wagon on the West Hill Road and no one came to look for me. I say it began that day, but maybe I'm wrong to say that. Maybe I should say the life I know now began nearly eight years later—when Overseer Flint brought the lunatic to the town poor farm.

1

The Gypsy Boy

Old Berthie was the one that told Jip. "A lunatic, boy," she said leaning so close Jip could count the hairs in her nostrils. "A raving lunatic." She sniffed. 'We're all of us poor and there be some," she rolled her eyes toward Old George and Sheldon Morse, "who is simple. But we're harmless, ain't we, boy? What do they mean bringing a lunatic amongst poor God-fearing folk who done no harm nor had no luck in this cruel world?"

Jip nodded solemnly. He never argued with Berthie. Once he dared question her when she said Ethan Allen had been a fool. After all, Ethan Allen and his Green Mountain Boys were the only genuine Vermont heroes Jip had ever heard tell of.

"Ethan Allen was a hero," he'd said.

She slapped him across the cheek so hard it stung. He wouldn't have credited that old wrinkled hand with such strength. "I said, 'fool,' boy. Don't go contradicting your elders!"

He didn't again. Besides, why *were* they bringing a lunatic to the poor farm?

"Money," Berthie said. "It'd cost the town too dear to send him to the asylum."

The Overseer of the Poor had appeared several days

earlier. Mr. Flint was an imposing man, tall enough to look down his nose at most of the population, with deep, buckshot eyes and sunken cheeks like a skeleton. You could tell from his frock coat and stovepipe hat what an important man he was in these parts. Indeed, he was the wealthiest and most important man that any of the residents knew of. It was he that had put each of them here on the town poor farm and demanded their gratitude on every possible occasion.

Overseer Flint drove his gig down the rutted road that morning in early April, cursing and whipping his mare, urging her through the spring mud. The residents, gathered respectfully in the yard to welcome his arrival, could hear the unchristian language from where they stood, huddled against one another for warmth. They reckoned the overseer above the law—even the biblical injunctions about the Lord's name—that tempered the speech of more ordinary mortals.

Despite the overseer's powerful tongue, the gig's left back wheel stuck, held fast in the greedy clay. "Jip, Sheldon, go help Mr. Flint," Otis Lyman, the farm's manager, yelled. Jip sprang forward, grabbing Sheldon's big, rough hand.

Sheldon looked at him, puzzled.

"We got to get the overseer's wheel loose, Sheldon. You and me together, ey?"

"Awright, Jip." Sheldon was always obliging. He just didn't catch on too fast.

The overseer stopped his red-faced cursing when the two of them got close.

"Good day to you, Mr. Flint, sir. I 'spect you better get down, sir," Jip said.

The overseer peered skeptically at them—the skinny boy and the husky young simpleton. The mare, straining at the reins, was sweating, her eyes wild from pulling. Couldn't the man see his own weight was making the wheel sink deeper and deeper?

"If'n you'd light down—" the boy began.

The man didn't wait for him to finish. His mouth pursed, he climbed down gingerly to the less muddy side, then threw his reins back toward Jip. Jip gathered them in one hand and watched as the tall man tiptoed around the muddiest ruts, picking a cautious way up the road to the crowd watching from the farmhouse yard.

"Wait, Sheldon," Jip said quietly when the man seemed out of earshot. "We got to make friends with this poor critter first. Mr. Flint has aggravated her something fearful with all his whipping and cursing." He moved to the mare's head and began to speak soothingly to the beast. The horse tossed her head once, but when the boy reached a chapped hand to her neck, she let him stroke it—barely stamping her muddy feet.

"Now, Sheldon," Jip said, his voice hardly louder than a spring breeze on a maple branch, "jest put your shoulder on that wheel, and when I say 'gee,' you shove, all right?"

Sheldon grinned, nodding his prematurely balding head. "I'm strong," he said proudly.

"That's right, Sheldon. You ain't got extra sense, but you're lots stronger than most anyone. I can't do without you. All I can do is talk sweet to this here horse. You're the one what's got to save the gig for the overseer."

"He'll say, 'Thank you, Sheldon. You're a good boy.' "

"He might, Sheldon. He jest might. Anyhow, we got to do it, thanks or no."

Lacking the overseer's weight and anger, and with Sheldon's strong shoulder against the wheel, the little mare eased the gig from its muddy trap with little effort. Jip patted her neck, kissed it, and praised her.

"You, too, Sheldon, you done every bit as good as the horse. Only she was upset, so I have to pet her special."

"I know, Jip."

They got no thanks from Mr. Flint. By the time horse, boy, and man had walked into the yard, and Jip had tied the reins to the hitching post, Mr. Flint had forgotten all about them. He was deep in a heated discussion with the farm manager, whose bulbous nose gleamed out redder than ever as he tried to argue with his superior. Mrs. Lyman was shooing all the residents into the house and out of hearing. "You, too, Jip, Sheldon. Everyone inside. None of your affair. The overseer has business with Mr. Lyman. Not with you." She was clucking like a mother hen and waving her arms at them. "We mustn't get in the gentlemen's way. Come on now."

They obeyed, if grudgingly. What could they do? They were like chicks here on this farm, pecking about to keep alive. There were seven of them at the time—four because they were old with no one to care for them: Berthie, Joe, Willis, and the silent Throsina. Two were simple—Sheldon in his early thirties and George, who was sickly and old and probably simple as well. Like Throsina, he seldom spoke, so no one could be quite sure.

And then there was Jip. When he arrived, Mr. Lyman had examined his teeth and pronounced that he was two, or maybe three, but no one knew for sure. He had fallen off the back of a wagon on the West Hill Road. Eyewitnesses (at least some who claimed to have been there on the usually deserted road) said the wagon was hellbent for hades, careening around the sharp curve about a mile out of the village when this odd bit of a boy just tumbled right off the back.

"No one bothered themselves to come back and claim you," Mrs. Lyman had said quite matter-of-factly.

"But didn't I tell you who I was?" Jip had figured early on that the maybe three-year-old child who fell off the wagon was old enough to tell somebody who he was.

"You were speaking nothing but gibberish at the time when you wasn't screaming your head off," she said. "Maybe you was a gypsy babe as some say. Or maybe you knocked your head on a stone when you hit the road." She cocked her head and studied him for a minute. "You ain't overly clever—not simple like Sheldon—but you likely lost something in that fall." She tapped her own head meaningfully.

Still, Jip was smart enough to wonder. There was plenty of time to ponder on things at the farm. He worked hard, as he and Sheldon were the only able-bodied residents, but most of the work left his mind free to ponder.

Why, he asked the chickens as he threw them grain, why had no one come back for him? Wouldn't you notice, say, if you began the day with six children and, come night, the count was down to five? Even if you were in a powerful hurry to leave these rocky hills to get West to where the good land lay, wouldn't it cross your mind to wonder what had become of your missing young'un that you once had but suddenly wasn't there anymore? Even a goose can count her goslings and know if a fox got one in the night.

Even supposing you were a heartless gypsy who stole other people's children like pies off a cooling sill, wouldn't you care about one of your own?

Jip's hair was darkish and on the curly side. His ears stuck out a bit. Did Romany ears protrude? The better to hear with—that was what he told Sheldon, but privately, staring into the wavy kitchen mirror, he thought they gave him the look of a two-handled jug. In the summer his skin burned dark and in the winter it was a perpetual shade of gray. But maybe that was because it didn't often get scrubbed. He was like a barn cat. He didn't mind giving himself a lick or two, but the sight of a tub of steaming water in the kitchen made him race toward the door. When he was tiny, Mrs. Lyman occasionally stripped him and doused him, but now that he was too big to haul about, she gave up on baths.

He might, indeed, be dark like a gypsy babe. On the other hand, perhaps, just perhaps, he was a child the Romanys had snatched from loving parents who were still mourning the loss of their beautiful baby boy.

Deacon Avery of the Congregational Church had come along the West Hill Road in his gig that day. He had gotten down and approached the child and told him to "go home" like he was some stray, but it hadn't worked. So after lengthy hesitation and debate with his wife, the deacon had picked the odd little screaming bundle off the dirt of the road.

His wife had made him take it direct to Reverend

Goodrich. The worthy reverend had thirteen children of his own and a very low salary. With some reluctance, he, in turn, had called upon the authorities—that is to say Mr. Flint, the Overseer of the Poor. It was the overseer's job to clear the town of tramps and transients and sweep the poor and mentally defective out of the village and onto the poor farm, where they would not offend the eyes and nostrils of God-fearing citizens, nor strain their purse strings overmuch.

Mr. Lyman had protested that the poor farm was not an orphan asylum, until Mr. Flint proposed that money could be extracted from the poor farm tax allocation to send the foundling to some distant institution. Or, alternatively, the child could be set up with a worthy Christian household closer by, again with fees from the poor farm budget. Mr. Lyman chose to keep his meager funds intact.

The farm manager prided himself that he had done well by the boy. He tried him in school once. But the other children complained of the smell, and even the little ones could make out the letters Jip could not. With so many citizens fleeing westward, tax revenues plummeted and with them funds to operate the poor farm. In desperation, the manager hired Jip out to a local farmer. To Mrs. Lyman's suggestion that Jip might be a bit too young for a hired man, he'd said the plain truth. "The boy is eating up all the profits, Mrs. Lyman." She couldn't argue. Even the boy, listening to the debate, knew the manager was right. For all his scrawniness, he shoveled in everything that wasn't nailed to the table. "But who will have him?" she'd asked.

Farmer Slaytor would. He would have anything he could beat and bully. His own dog cowered at the sight of him. Jip's most vivid memory of that time was being grabbed by an ear and dragged to see how badly he had swept the kitchen or shoveled out the barn. "See! See!" the man would yell. "A blind idjit could do better." As Jip swept and cried, the dog would find him and rub his body against the boy's legs and whimper its sympathy.

Jip might be there yet—one ear larger than the other from all that yanking—but Farmer Slaytor upped and married a husky widow woman from Chelsea and sent his less than satisfactory hand back to the poor farm.

To Jip it felt like coming home. For the poor farm was the only home he could remember. He loved the rocky pastures. He loved standing in the spring wind, gazing at the distant hills, the green deeply pockmarked with the gray of Deacon Avery's granite quarry and the piles of slag around it. He loved the way the sun glinted off the stone. Perhaps, when he was a man, he would go to work there, driving shivs into the rock face with a great sledge-hammer, filling the holes with black powder, and BOOM! blasting the huge granite blocks from the bedrock.

When he came back to the poor farm after those few months away, he seemed a different boy. Privately, Mr. Lyman wondered why Slaytor had let him go. He wouldn't, of course, have said anything to anyone, for it was the poor who were to be grateful, not their managers. Lyman fancied himself not a fully healthy man, and the beasts and residents of the farm were a constant trial to him. The boy had a way with both, though. He was scarcely more than half the height of summer corn, but the flock of scrawny merino sheep would see him coming across the pasture and lope awkwardly over the hill to meet him. His front teeth were hardly out and in again, yet he was milking old Bonnie twice a day, and somehow, the milk she had been so stingy with— however Mrs. Lyman tugged and yanked—flowed like a fountain under his small hands. And that year, instead of her usual stillbirth, old Bonnie bore a calf alive and healthy enough for Lyman to sell at a nice profit, a bit of which bought him some tobacco and a bottle of medicinal spirits to augment his store of homemade cider fermenting in the cellar.

How much of the manager's secret thoughts Jip knew or sensed it would be hard to say, but he was not dissatisfied with his life. Still, he was a normal boy and curious about a number of things. At the moment, he wished it was his ear against the door and not Mrs. Lyman's. He'd like to know what the overseer was saying about the mysterious lunatic.

"Jip!"

He came out of his daydream with a start. Mrs. Lyman jerked her head to summon him close. He left the cluster of residents at the stove and came around the big table to where she stood. "Mr. Lyman will be wanting you," she said. "But, first, go out to the pump and put a rag to your face. Mercy, boy, the overseer has come calling. We run a clean establishment around here. How will he know that if you go talking to him with a face like a pig snout?"

Jip retraced his steps around the table. He was at the east door and ready to go out when she stopped him.

"Take Sheldon and wash his face, too, you hear?" Jip returned to the stove side, taking Sheldon's big hand in his own. "And get his ears this time," she called out after the two of them.

"Why does Mr. Flint want to see me, Jip? Have I been bad?"

"Bend over, Sheldon. I got to reach your ears."

"Have I, Jip?"

"Naa-h. I don't know but what he's got a job of work for you and me."

"You and me, right, Jip? You and me together?"

Jip nodded. "All right, you can straighten up now, Sheldon. You scrub up pretty as a heifer in a county fair."

Sheldon looked troubled. "Is that a joke, Jip?"

"Ehyuh."

The young man laughed, showing his gaggle of decayed and missing teeth. Jip smiled, rinsing out the rag and then working a little harder than usual on his own face. He took Sheldon's hand and they presented themselves for Mrs. Lyman's inspection. Mrs. Lyman opened the main kitchen door.

As they came into the yard, the two men turned. "A cage," Mr. Lyman said, "a cage, Jip. We need a cage."

Jip didn't ask what for, although he wanted to. The overseer's presence made him shy. "How big?" he asked.

The manager turned to Mr. Flint. "Oh," the tall man said, "about as tall as I am—say, six feet cubed, that should do it without waste. Do you know what a cube is, boy?"

"Yessir."

"But strong. It will need to be very strong." He looked

doubtfully at Jip—up and down as if measuring his height. "Perhaps we should hire it done, Mr. Lyman."

Mr. Lyman was alarmed. "And *pay* to have it done? Above the cost of materials—which will be considerable?"

"Yes, well," the overseer said. "But it must be strong. You'll need to buy iron hinges and a padlock."

"I ain't hardly the budget for such expensive—"

"If we send him to Brattleboro it would take your entire appropriation, Mr. Lyman. Believe me, next town meeting, you'd be out of a job altogether."

Mr. Lyman looked beaten. "The boy and I can do it," he said.

"Sheldon can help, can't I, Jip? Can't I?"

"Sure, Sheldon," Jip said gently, "no one here could get along without you."

"Humph." The overseer untied his horse, and watching his feet in their fancy boots to avoid the mud wherever possible, he walked his mare and wagon back to the main road.

The next afternoon, as soon as Mr. Lyman could fetch the rock maple slats from the lumberyard and the hardware from Peck's store in the village, Jip and Sheldon set about building a cage for the lunatic.

2

The Lunatic

Jip put the straw mattress Mrs. Lyman had made on one side of the cage, sat down, and pulled shut the slat door. He wanted to know how it might feel to live in a cage. There was a chamber pot in the corner. He had made a little trapdoor so it could be taken out and emptied and food could be passed in without having to undo the padlock on the main entry. He looked about, taking in the smell of the new-shaved wood. He and Sheldon had done a good job of it. It felt clean and, well, cozy. It might be nice to have a place of his own like this, away from the snoring of the old men and Sheldon's tossing and restless sleep talk. Well, at least he had a cot of his own now. At first he'd had to sleep with Sheldon and woke up on the floor more mornings than not.

He supposed he'd have slept on the floor the rest of his days, but a lucky thing happened. A year back Old Man Rutherford died, and Jip grabbed the vacant cot before Mrs. Lyman had time even to wash out the raggedy quilt.

He stretched out on the mattress. The straw pricked through the ticking and his thin shirt and britches, but it smelled fresh, unlike his own musty bed. The plank floor of the cage was no harder than the wooden frame of his cot. He sucked in a deep, satisfied breath, gazing up at the strips of wood that he and Sheldon had nailed across the top. Mr. Lyman had grumbled about the waste of nails, which came dear at a penny apiece, but the overseer had demanded that they triple-nail each end of every slat.

It was like looking at the ceiling through an elaborate fence. The sides—the same crisscrossed pattern as the top—felt like a protection. He couldn't ever remember having privacy, even at Slaytor's he had slept in the same room as the farmer. Privacy, or the desire for it, was not an idea that he could put into words. But in the cage he sensed what it might feel like to have a little space all one's own that no other, not even simple, sweet Sheldon or his beloved animals, would intrude upon.

"Jip! Ji—yip!" The boy sighed and left the comfort of the cage to respond to Mrs. Lyman's cry. What he needed was a cage with walls so thick that he wouldn't be able to hear the constant call of his name.

They brought the lunatic that very afternoon. Once more the residents stood shivering in the April chill, watching a horse wagon come up the road. This time, neither Jip nor Sheldon was sent to help. Unlike the gig, this wagon was pulled by a strong team of Morgans, and besides the driver and the overseer on the front seat, four sturdy townsmen sat at the corners of the wagon bed surrounding a strange bent-over figure whose screams could be heard long before any face or recognizable human form came into focus.

"Jeezums Crow!" Old Joe exclaimed, revealing that even a man half deaf could hear the commotion. Sheldon clamped both hands over his ears and squeezed his eyes shut, trying to keep out the terrifying sound.

When at last the wagon pulled into the yard, Jip could

see that the strange form in the center of the wagon bed was a man, with only his head free. A rope wound about his legs and back, bringing his knees to his chest. His arms were around his legs and his huge, gnarled hands were tied together at the wrists. The rough hemp rope had rubbed the flesh raw, and between his shrieks, he would duck his shaggy head to bite at the rope with large, yellow teeth.

The hair was appalling—long as a woman's—but it seemed all of a piece with his beard, both of which were streaked with gray and dotted with spittle.

Sheldon opened his eyes long enough to take in the sight, then grabbed Jip's arm in terror. "It's all right, Sheldon," Jip whispered. "I won't let him hurt you," which was the emptiest promise he'd ever made. The man looked quite determined to burst his bonds and do damage to the whole lot of them.

The four townsmen jumped off the back of the wagon before the driver had halted the team. They were all shouting orders. But the yells of the overseer (in his gardening clothes instead of his frock coat) were louder than even the ravings of the lunatic. "Carry it to the cage!"

Two of the townsmen were up on the wagon trying to shove the lunatic over the side to the other two. It couldn't be done. They called for help, so Jip disentangled himself from Sheldon's anxious grasp and scrambled up to help them lift the trussed creature over the side like a bag of rocks into the arms of the men below. They swayed almost to their knees, cursing at the weight. Then shoving, pushing, and stumbling, they carried him into the house, Mrs. Lyman scurrying ahead to open the doors and the overseer shouting out orders. The lunatic, with all his limbs secured, squirmed and bleated like a hog set for the slaughter.

The men dragged and dumped him in the cage, tripping over the madman's body in their hurry to escape. Mr. Flint slammed the door, clamped the great iron padlock together with a clunk of metal, and turned to present the key to Mr. Lyman. The manager's wide eyes were so fixed on the lunatic that it was several moments and a jab before he saw the key to take it.

"Mind you, take care, Lyman," the overseer said to the manager, who was visibly shaking. "I hold you responsible."

The escorts did not even stay for the cups of hard cider that Mrs. Lyman had poured out earlier. They hurried to the wagon and left the farm as fast as the horses could take them down the muddy track.

"Wal," said Mrs. Lyman, downing a cup of cider, "waste not, want not." She handed a cup to her husband who, without a word, hastily downed two more. Between them they finished off the six cups prepared for the visitors, while the thirsty residents stood by, licking their dry lips.

All but Jip, who, seeing the Lymans occupied, stole the butcher knife and crept back to the room next to the shed where the old lunatic lay. His shrieks had quieted to rhythmic moans.

"Sh-sh-hush, there," Jip said. "Hush, old fellow. We ain't going to hurt you."

For a moment the groaning ceased, and the old man struggled about to fix his bloodshot gaze toward the bars where Jip knelt, crooning. "Can you roll yourself to the side?" the boy asked softly. "Or jest swing close enough for me to cut them ropes for you?" He spoke in the voice he used for Sheldon and George and the poor dumb beasts in his care. Miraculously, the lunatic seemed to understand. With an enormous lunge, he heaved his body against the slats.

The trick was to get the rope cut without giving the lunatic a chance to grab the knife. Sweat stood out on Jip's forehead as he eased the blade through the slats and under the ropes across the man's back. He crooned as he sawed at the ropes. "There, there. It'll be better soon. There. That's the main one. A minute more and I'll have your ankles free."

The lunatic stretched out his cramped limbs, crying a bit with the pain of it.

"Now, can you jest move around to the front?" The man hesitated, trying to unravel the request. "Come close, here to me. Stick those old hands through the slats. Then I can cut loose your wrists, too." He put his own wrists together trying to signal to the man what was needed.

The lunatic shuffled about on his knees, then stretched out his bound hands. He could barely squeeze them through the slats. He flinched slightly as Jip worked the blade between his wrists. "Steady now, quiet. I'd be loath to slice you instead of the rope."

The lunatic obeyed. A little doglike whimper had replaced the moans.

Jip smiled. "See, it's near cut through now. You'll feel lots better without this rope grazing your poor old flesh. There. See?"

The man pulled his hands back into the cage, turning them over as if to study them.

"Maybe I should get you some ointment to put on those rope burns. Want I should do that?"

The man nodded, rubbing first one sore wrist and then the other. His lips parted, showing his great yellow teeth. At first Jip was startled. It took him a moment to understand. The lunatic was smiling. Jip smiled back, shyly at first, but as the lunatic's smile broadened, so did his own.

"There," he said. "Well. I got to fetch the ointment. Don't fuss while I'm gone, old fellow. I won't be long."

"What are you doing with my knife?" Mrs. Lyman was a bit tipsy from her two cups of cider, which she had downed too fast for a woman unaccustomed to fermented drinks.

"I figured Mr. Lyman would want me to cut the lunatic loose. The poor fellow trussed up like a pig ready to be stuck. It weren't human to leave him so."

"He's hardly human, that one," she said.

"I need some ointment—the rope has rubbed his wrists to bleeding."

She fetched the ointment from her cabinet of assorted medications. It was right behind the medicinal spirits.

"You aren't afraid of the creature?" she asked, her back still to the boy.

He shrugged. What was the answer? Maybe he was and maybe he wasn't. He only knew the lunatic needed to have his limbs loosed and his wounds attended to. "I don't figure he'll take unkind to having his wrists soothed."

She turned then and gave him a look before she continued in a sterner tone. "Well, don't forget you've got chores to attend to," she said. "They don't stop just 'cause you've found yourself a new pet."

"I won't," he said and sighed. That was how he had acquired responsibility for all the farm's livestock and the neediest residents. They were "Jip's pets," which out of the goodness of the manager's heart, the boy was allowed to care for.

The cage room was quiet when Jip pushed open the door. He wished he'd scrubbed down the walls after he'd carried all the years of trash out of it yesterday. It seemed so dark in the small room. A high north window let in little light, and the soot on the walls, evidence of the faulty fireplace, made the room even more dingy. The cage filled more than half the space. Beside it there was no furniture. It was a gloomy place to spend one's days. The lunatic was lying stretched out on his mattress. It was too short for him, so his feet hung off the end. The man was staring at the slats, which patterned his view of the cracked ceiling plaster.

"How came I here?" he asked without moving his head.

"What?" Jip would have been less startled to hear Bible verses coming from old Bonnie's bovine muzzle.

"How came I into this cage?" His words were clear, no relation to the ravings of a lunatic.

"You was carried here, sir, on Mr. Flint's wagon."

"The Overseer of the Poor, Mr. Flint?"

"Yessir."

"And does Mr. Flint aim to keep me in a cage like some beast from the jungle?"

The boy hung his head, ashamed to be one of those who had carried the man in here.

"You was raving, sir, somewhat wild and mad. I reckon it was for your safety."

The man sighed deeply and sat up to face him.

"I—I brung you ointment, sir, for your wrists. The rope scraped them something awful."

Again the man raised his hands, turning them over to examine the wounds, as though he'd forgotten.

"If you'll stick them through the slats, I can rub some of this on them—soothe them a bit?" His voice went up into a question as if addressing an elder whose preferences must now be consulted.

The man stuck one large hand through the slats. "You're a kind young feller. What's your name?"

"Jip, sir."

"My friends used to call me Put," the old man said. "I'd like it if you'd call me Put. It's for Putnam, but that's too grand a name for the likes of me, don't you think?"

Jip grinned. "Put's nice," he said.

"Why Jip?"

"Mr. Lyman dubbed me Jip," he said, gently massaging the cold ointment into the raw flesh. "On account of I fell off the back of a wagon and some says it was a gypsy wagon."

"I see." Put pulled the left hand back and thrust out the right. "This is the town farm then?"

"Yessir." He was a little sorry to be the one to give such news. "To save you from being sent to the asylum, it was."

The man didn't remark on that, and Jip decided not to say that the cage was the town's way of saving taxpayer money. The man's plight was harsh enough.

"I don't reckon . . ." the man began. "I don't reckon they'd let me take a bath . . . or—" he laughed shortly "—or trim my hair and beard?"

"Likely not." Jip kept his head over his task, avoiding the man's eyes. "They're a bit jumpy, yet. You jest got here less than an hour ago. . . . Maybe when you settle in more . . . There. Does that ease it some?"

The man pulled back his hand. "It does. You're a good lad. Could you make it one more favor? A wet cloth to wipe my face?"

Before the week was out, Jip had cajoled Mr. Lyman into letting him fill a tub in Put's room, so the man could bathe. And although no one, not even Jip, wanted to hand over a straight razor, Jip was allowed scissors to cut Put's wild growth of hair and beard to a more becoming human length.

"Do you like a pleasing tune, my boy?"

"I don't know. I'm not much for music. All I ever heard was hymns in church and most of them is pretty drear."

The man began to sing, then. He had a high voice, clear like sleigh bells across the snow.

As the days passed, Jip came to know that song well, for Put would sing it over and over, never tiring of either the melody or the words. Sometimes Jip would try to sing along, " 'All is well, all is well,' " though his own voice sounded scratchy and tuneless compared to the lunatic's sweet song.

In truth, Jip could scarcely call Put a lunatic. He was not an unhandsome man when bathed, his clothes scrubbed by Jip, his hair and beard neat. His eyes had quite lost their bloodshot wildness.

Put's lunacy had fled or been cast into some distant

swine like in the Bible tale. Every night Jip longed to leave the cage unlocked, for it made his heart sick to clap a padlock against his newfound friend.

"You daren't leave it open, boy," Put said. "If I go raving in the night, I can't think what harm this wretched mind might betray me to."

So, reluctantly, Jip slammed the padlock's shackle into its case and hung the key in the medicine cabinet behind the medicinal spirits.

Then without warning one night, the house awoke to shrieks and terrible banging. Jip threw on his britches and raced down the stairs, his suspenders flying.

"Put, Put," he cried, to make himself heard over the din. But his friend paid no heed to his pleading and hurled his body against the slats until Jip felt sure he would tear all the nails from their holes and splinter the rock maple timbers into kindling.

"Put, Put," he murmured, half crying out his friend's name. "There's no one here would harm you. Rest, rest, hush, don't punish your poor self so—"

In answer Put tore at his face until the blood ran and soiled his shirt.

The Lymans and the residents, all in their nightclothes, stood about in the hallway, terrified to cross the threshold. Only Jip dared approach the cage, but even he stood back lest the lunatic's great hand dart out at him through the slats.

"Come back," Jip crooned. "Don't let the devil possess you. Come back. It's me, your old friend, Jip, what you sings and talks to."

Jip sat on the cold floor, clasped his hands about his knees, and began to sing:

21

"... I soon shall be
From ev'ry pain and sorrow free.
I shall the King of glory see,
All is well, all is well!"

He sang until his throat was hoarse, not loud—he knew that he could not sing above the lunatic's threats and curses—but, rocking his body, he sang on to comfort himself. He had the vain hope that somewhere in that terrible head behind those fearful teeth a bit of the Put he cared for was still alive and could hear that Jip was near and would not desert him.

At some point well past daylight both the madman and the boy fell into exhausted sleep.

Jip was awakened by Mrs. Lyman's call from the hallway. He must get his lazy self to the barn and milk, she said. He stole away from the huge form lying crammed into a corner of the cage, splattered with blood and spittle and worse.

Old Bonnie welcomed him with a gentle low and a barely impatient stomp of her back hoof. "I know, my darling," he said sorrowfully. "I'm late and causing you discomfort. But how could I leave him? And then—" he pulled the stool closer and rested his head against her warm flank "—and then I fell to sleep." He began the rhythmic stroking of her teats, and as the milk *plinked* into the waiting pail, he remembered his sad and desperate singing in the night. He had found a beast he couldn't tame at will. It was like to break his young heart.

3

Newcomers

Put came to himself later that day, but the residents were now more wary of him. Sheldon grabbed Jip's arm and begged him not to go into the cage room. He cried like a child when Jip persisted. Jip never wanted to hurt Sheldon, but Put was—well, he was Put and he belonged to Jip in a way no one else ever had.

There was no way of knowing when one of the spells would come over the man. Whenever Put was out of the cage for even the briefest time, the anxious twittering about of the manager and his wife tainted any small taste of freedom Jip could offer to his friend.

Only Jip remained faithful, daring, when the weather was fair, to take Put out as far as the pasture so that he could feel the sun on his face and welcome the slow approach of Vermont spring.

There were new lambs to count, and, as if to dispel her luckless reputation once and for all, Bonnie dropped yet another healthy calf, a heifer at that.

Put continued in his right mind through the end of April and right on into early May. Perhaps the lengthening of the days cheered his troubled soul, for he sang his songs and played upon a wooden pipe he'd told Jip how to fashion, as he was never allowed anything sharper than his pewter spoon.

He was in his peaceful phase the afternoon the Widow Wilkens appeared, her three unhappy children in tow. Jip's heart danced to see more children come to the farm, having been for all his life there the only one. The oldest was even near to his own size, though a girl. The next was a bit of a boy, just coming into speech, and the youngest a baby girl, still on the breast.

The widow's husband had been, Berthie informed them all, the town's most notorious drunk. Then, during the last big snow, he fell on his way home and froze to death in a snow drift. An empty bottle for illegal spirits was found nearby. No one counted his death much of a loss, though Jip wondered if his wife and children had. They surely might. Still, the taxpayers soon felt the pinch, for the drunkard had left nothing behind save debts, so the responsibility for his family's care fell upon the town.

Jip ran out to meet the newcomers with delight—a delight that was met with cold stares from everyone except for a shy smile from the little boy.

"Show the Wilkenses the empty room next to the gentlemen's quarters," Mrs. Lyman said primly. "Gentlemen" was not a word she was accustomed to use to describe the male residents of the farm.

"Jest follow me, then," Jip called out, running up the stairs. He turned at the top to watch the labored ascent of the new residents.

Lucy, the girl, was carrying a large carpetbag, bumping it from step to step, while her mother juggled the baby on her right hip and dragged the little boy upward with her left hand. "Lift your feet, Toddy, for mercy's sake, jest lift your feet."

Jip went back down, thinking at least to help Lucy with the huge bag, but when he reached for the handles, she snatched it away. "It's ours!" she said, as though he had been intent on stealing it from her.

"I jest thought to give you a hand with it," he said, confused.

"You have a monstrous dirty face."

Jip shook his head and climbed back up to the landing. He didn't tell her that her face wasn't so clean either. Why should he? He knew a hurting animal when he saw one. There was no need to pain her further.

At the supper table, which filled the center of the drab kitchen, the widow and her children sat huddled together at the far side near Mrs. Lyman. The little boy's nose hardly scraped the splintery tabletop. Mr. Lyman served the bowls of mush from the kettle and passed them down. Lucy looked at hers, her face twisting as though she felt nauseous. Her mother poked both her and Toddy and bent to say something sharp and low. Reluctantly, both children picked up their spoons. Jip didn't wait to see how much they ate, he only waited until he had Put's bowl and took it with a spoon down the hall to the cage room.

"Here you are, Put." Jip passed the bowl and spoon through the trapdoor. "Hot at least."

The old man sniffed the steaming mush. "Ah, one of Mrs. Lyman's culinary triumphs." When he smiled like that, his teeth didn't seem so large and menacing.

"We got new residents." Put counted on Jip to bring the news of the world outside the cage room. "A Widow Wilkens and her young 'uns. Berthie says the mister died in the March storm."

"There's unluckier people in this world than you nor me, Jip," the old man said, settling back against the slats with his supper.

"I reckon." It was a new thought to Jip. He never regarded himself as lucky or unlucky. He was just Jip, just here. But he had pitied his friend—a lunatic and a pauper to boot. Was Put right? Was it unluckier still to be the orphan child of a drunken father? Jip returned to the big kitchen table and his own cool mush, determined to be especially kind to the prickly Lucy.

"Make him stop looking at me, Ma," Lucy whispered hoarsely.

In answer Mrs. Wilkens reached past Toddy and gave Lucy's face a slap. "Mind your manners, girl."

Yes, thought Jip. There's some that's unluckier than me.

He felt truly lucky a few days later. He was going into town. A trip into the village for anything besides Sunday services at the Congregational Church was always something of an adventure. Jip liked to study the variety of horses and people on the busy street, to hear the rattle of wagons, the call of greetings. He wished for a cap. If he had a cap to tip, he could have joined in the proper "Howdy-do's" and "Good morning to you's" and made a wise pronouncement on the weather.

Since the day that Lucy had made mention of his face, he had taken more care to splash cold water on it and wipe it carefully on the tail of his shirt. This day he looked down at the raw, red hands sticking out of his skimpy sleeves and washed them as well. There was no mirror over the pump, only the wavy one over the kitchen sink, but he ran his fingers through his tangled curls and patted them to his head. There. At least he felt handsomer.

"Where you off to?" Lucy had come out to the pump.

"Me and Mr. Lyman got to take the heifer in to sell." He lowered his voice. "I got to help. The man's got no way with critters."

"Oh." He tried to figure if she was wanting to go too, but he knew Mr. Lyman wouldn't allow it. He wouldn't even let Sheldon go into town on errands. "I can't be bothered taking care of the idjit," he'd say when Jip begged on Sheldon's behalf, knowing how Sheldon did so love to go places. Though in truth, it would be Jip taking care of both beast and man.

The road was rutted, but the mud was hard, and if Mr. Lyman guided Old Jack around the worst of the ruts, there should be no delay traveling on such a beautiful morning. Jip, sitting in the bed of the wagon, stroked the heifer's neck and half talked, half sang to keep her quiet. In a way, he was sad to see her go, but the sale would help out with the finances of the farm, now seriously strained with the addition of Put and the Wilkens family to the population.

It wasn't hard to tell when money was tight. The meals, meager at best, degenerated into a steady diet of mush, accompanied by a stream of complaints flowing from the head of the table to the foot and back again.

In the good old days, as Mr. Lyman often reminded

them, the able-bodied of the poor would have been let out to the highest bidder and would have brought a good bit of money to the town instead of draining the town purse. But, some do-gooders claimed this practice smacked too close to southern slavery, so they began to put out the poor to the lowest bidder—the householder who proposed to take on the responsibility for the pauper at least expense to the town. This practice, alas, fell into disfavor as the ever vigilant do-gooders sniffed out cases of abuse and claimed near starvation. So out of Christian charity the town had purchased for their benefit—*for their benefit*—this wonderful farm and had hired the Lymans to manage it and the lives of all those unfortunate paupers for whom the town must be responsible.

But, and at this point the manager invariably sighed, the task of keeping the farm from becoming an undue tax burden on those same generous citizens fell entirely to him. Mr. Flint, the Overseer of the Poor, cared for nothing but balanced books and an unruffled citizenry. And how, pray tell, was Mr. Lyman supposed to make the farm pay for itself with only two able-bodied males among the residents—one of them a boy of unknown age who could not or would not succeed when he was hired out and the other a simpleton?

Jip would have felt more guilt or even more sympathy if the manager himself had been more industrious. After all, he seemed perfectly able-bodied, if a bit on the plump side. He was neither young nor simple. But Jip supposed himself only an ignorant boy and not up to understanding the problems of his elders.

The sun warmed Jip's head and shoulders. Winter was

nearly gone at last, and though a May snow was not unknown, it wasn't likely. He hardly minded that by June he would be at work from dawn to dusk. He was not a stranger to work. Sometimes he racked his brains to recall who had done the milking, plowing, seeding, cultivating, picking, and reaping before Mr. Lyman determined that Sheldon had the muscles and Jip had the sense to carry out all these tasks.

Still, he could enjoy a rare holiday from work. He longed to stretch out full length in the wagon and bathe in the sunlight. He was sleepy. He'd hardly had a full night's rest since Put came. Often he slept by the cage, in case the lunatic got to raving in the night. Was it true what Berthie said about the full moon making him crazier? Jip couldn't be sure. Put's bad spells didn't seem as regular as the phases of the moon. And it certainly didn't take a full moon to unhinge him. At least Put was less agitated when the sun was shining, and summer with its long golden days was sure to come.

The wagon hit a bump in the rutted road. Mr. Lyman grunted a curse word and smacked the reins against Jack's patient back. The calf gave a startled little bleat.

"Sh-shhh," Jip whispered. "You ain't going to slaughter. No need to fear. Someone's going to buy you for a nice milk cow. You're a little beauty, I tell you. You'll live to a ripe old cow age, you will."

The little heifer twisted her neck to look up at him with worshipful brown eyes. He did love a calf. When Bonnie delivered a stillborn, it tore him apart, even though, with no calf to nurse, it meant more milk, butter, and cheese for the residents.

They were approaching the edge of the village. As always, he stared at the large houses as they passed. Curtains made the houses look plump and sleepy-eyed as they sat comfortably amongst their luxuriant shade trees. What did people do in the village? They couldn't all work in the mill or the livery stable or at the harness makers. They didn't seem to keep chickens much less a cow, and, aside from the few garden plots, which had not yet been planted, it was hard to see how the rich ate, let alone how they prospered.

Overseer Flint, for example, was called a banker. Jip had even seen the so-called bank, a squat one-story clapboard structure near the village green. But what did people *do* in banks? He knew it was somehow related to money, but what? You didn't grow money. Why would you need a building for it when a mattress or jar or even a drawer would be much more handy?

A visitor to the poor farm years ago had, upon leaving, handed Jip a copper penny. Since it was the only money the boy had ever possessed, he always carried it with him in the pocket of his trousers. The donor had said to Jip: "Now save this, my boy. A penny saved is a penny earned." So Jip had obediently saved it, but it hadn't earned him any more. Jip couldn't figure for the life of him how the man had thought it might. A penny wasn't a hen that could hatch a bunch of copper chicks.

Once, last fall, when he happened to be in the village, he had come close to spending his penny. Peck's store had candies, all different shiny colors, and they were ten for one penny. He was sorely tempted. Those ten candies would give him and Sheldon at least five days of pleasure. But the visitor's warning had stopped him. This particular penny must be destined for greater things than sweets for him and Sheldon to suck.

They were nearly at Peck's now, but the wagon didn't stop. First, they would deliver the heifer on the far side of the village and get the payment for it. Then, perhaps, Mr. Lyman would stop at the store. Jip hoped so. He loved to see the bright candies in their glass jars lined up like a row of rich village girls in their Sunday calicoes. Looking was free and did no harm.

He lifted the calf down from the wagon, nearly falling under the weight of it. Mr. Lyman was in his good suit and couldn't be expected to handle livestock. Jip bent over and gave the calf a secret good-bye kiss and then climbed back up into the wagon.

Mr. Lyman did stop at the store, but to Jip's disappointment, he ordered the boy to stay with the horse while he ran his errand. Jip clambered up to the wagon seat, leaving the reins loose across Jack's broad back and watched as the manager climbed the steps. Just as Mr. Lyman reached the entrance, a man came out, and the two of them dodged each other in the doorway with bows and nods. Jip gazed longingly at the storefront, his mouth all set for the candies he imagined his penny might have fetched.

For a second, the stranger's eyes met his own. The man looked startled, then, shifting his gaze, came down the steps and over to the wagon.

"Waiting for your papa?" he asked. There was something sticky and syrupy about the man's tone that made Jip want to lie, but the sin of lying was too heavy for his conscience, so he shook his head.

"Your . . . uncle?"

Why did the man care who Mr. Lyman was? Besides, he ought to know without asking. Everyone knew Mr. Lyman.

"No kin, eh?"

Jip neither nodded nor shook his head, but turned away to stare at a wagon passing on the road. The stranger was nosy and rude. He had no business asking such questions. Best to ignore him.

"Where you living, sonny?" The man waited, and when Jip failed to answer, added impatiently, "No cause to be unmannerly. I'm just making friendly conversation, you know."

Jip didn't know. That was the point. The man's words didn't seem friendly at all. To his great relief, Mr. Lyman came out of the store soon after, already stuffing his newly purchased tobacco into his pipe. Jip handed him the reins and climbed back to the wagon bed, being careful not to look down at the stranger, who had yet to move away.

"Your pardon, good sir—" Mr. Lyman ignored this greeting, clicked a command to the horse, and with a slap of the reins pulled away, leaving the man standing there red-faced and openmouthed.

"Who was that stranger you was talking to, boy?" the manager asked as they left the village.

"I wasn't talking, sir. He was. He was asking me if I was some relation to you."

The idea clearly displeased the manager. "Don't make up to strangers, boy."

"No, sir. It warn't his business if we was kin or no. Which we are not."

"He's not been in these parts before. What's he doing around here?"

"That I don't know. I didn't tell him nothing, sir."

Mr. Lyman gave a grunt and said no more.

Still, when Jip and Sheldon came in from the hen-house next afternoon, there was the stranger having a cup of tea and biscuits with Mrs. Lyman, right there in the farmhouse kitchen. The stranger must have found out from someone where the wagon had come from. It seemed unlikely to Jip that he had made his way out to the farm by accident. The town farm wasn't what you could call on the road to anywhere else.

The man raised his eyes as the two of them opened the door. Jip caught the man giving him a quick once-over, but he turned right back to Mrs. Lyman, chatting about the prospects for a late frost as though he and the manager's wife were old friends.

Jip washed the eggs and put them carefully into the basket. He wondered if Mr. Lyman knew that the stranger was poking his nose into the very kitchen of the farmhouse. The boy shivered. There was something wrong: The unknown man from the store now chittering away in the kitchen, having himself a cup of the manager's tea as though he was some welcomed and very familiar guest. Not even a parlor visitor—a kitchen one.

"Come on, Sheldon," he said. They left the room as fast as Jip could pull Sheldon out. Jip kept clear of the house until he saw the stranger well on the road toward the village.

He was a tall man, close to Mr. Flint's height, dressed in dark, formal-looking clothes, and walking, not heavy like a farmer, or even proud like a banker, but like a kind of—well, one night Jip had seen a weasel slinking around the chicken house looking for a hole to slide through. It was sort of like that.

The man stopped, looking back up the road toward the farmhouse. Jip jerked out of sight behind the shed.

4

Beware the Stranger

That night Jip waited until the meal was done and everyone had left the table before he took in Put's supper. Then he settled himself down beside the cage. It wasn't so much that he wanted to confide in his friend as he needed Put to help him sort out his own confusion.

"Why you reckon he wanted to know if Mr. Lyman was my pa or any kin? Everyone knows who Mr. Lyman is and that he don't have children—nor would he want a gypsy throwaway mistook for his own flesh and blood."

"You're a good lad, Jip, gypsy or no."

"Well, you and me is friends, Put, and I thank you for it, but what I want to know is why sudden like this stranger pops into town, asks me and Mr. Lyman nosy questions which we are too smart to answer, and next thing he's in the kitchen chatting up the missus like they was old-time acquaintances."

"Strange," Put agreed.

"Powerful strange, I say."

"Did it strike you, Jip—now, mind, I never laid eyes on the feller—but did it come to mind that he might think he knows you?"

"Well, he don't."

"I mean from before—that he might know who you belonged to before you fell off that particular wagon?"

"But I was a wee thing, still wobbly on my legs. How would anyone recognize me after all these years? And what if he did? Couldn't he have just said so straight out? Not sniff around like a hound on a trail?"

"Strange," Put repeated.

"If he thought he know'd me," Jip persisted, "how come he don't ask right out, tell me what he had in mind?"

"It would seem the natural, honest thing . . ."

"Well, whatever he is, he ain't honest, Put. I shouldn't be in the way of judging my feller man, but there is something smells very far from fresh about that feller. It gives me the tremblies seeing him in our kitchen. You know something else? Mrs. Lyman never told the mister that he was here."

"No?"

"Not a word passed down the length of that supper table tonight, Put. She says to him like she does every time he goes to the village, 'What is the news in town, Mr. Lyman?' And he says through his slurps, like always, 'Not much, Mrs. Lyman.' And she don't give him any news of the day here a-tall. Visitors is news, Put. You can count on it, visitors of any kind is news, and strangers is enough to call the county press."

"Not a word, eh?"

"Not one little word. Like she was keeping it secret that the stranger come, though he was drinking the tea and eating up the biscuits and Mr. Lyman is sure to notice when he takes to counting stock. He is powerful particular about things that come missing in the count."

"You must be careful, Jip. I don't think this stranger is after Mrs. Lyman's biscuits."

"If he is, he must be near to starvation."

They shared a laugh. Even to those whose memory of tasty vittles was nonexistent or near dead, Mrs. Lyman's cooking was a subject of scorn.

Still, how was Jip to be wary when he didn't know from what direction danger came, if at all? The tremblies persisted for a day or two—once or twice he imagined a figure coming up the road—but there was no one, and life returned to its natural rhythms.

But not quite. For the Widow Wilkens and her children had stirred the still pond of the farm. No one could deny it.

Jip felt responsible for Lucy and Toddy. He could safely leave the cub to her dam, but the other two needed him. Lucy pretended to ignore him, but the little boy took to following him around like a puppy. One day Jip was headed to the far pasture to see if any ewes had dropped lambs during the night and he was startled by the sound of crying. He turned around. Small Toddy was lying on his face in the prickly grass, kicking and screaming. Jip ran back to him, alarmed.

"Too fast!" the child screamed at him. "Too fast!"

"Sorry, little feller. I didn't know you was trotting after." He picked the child up, brushed off the dirt, and swung him to his shoulders. "Here. That better?"

The child shrieked with delight. "Giddap!" he cried, smacking Jip's cheek with his small hand. "Giddap, Jack!"

"Hold tight, now!" As he broke into a canter, he spotted Lucy. She had come running out of the house, after her brother, he supposed, and was standing there watching, a scowl twisting her face.

"C'mon, Lucy!" Toddy yelled.

"Yeah, come on. We're off to see if any lambs were born last night." She shrugged and turned, as if to go in. "Aw, come with us." She didn't move, so he cantered away with Toddy clutching his hair and squealing with anxious joy.

There was a new one—a little black-face love—that bleated so dear and nudged its ma for milk.

Jip swung Toddy gently to the ground. "Shh," he said. "She don't know you yet." The ewe eyed Toddy with suspicion and began to move away, much to the distress of the lamb, who wobbled after her, crying as it went. Toddy made to run after them, but Jip caught him around the waist. "Wait here. See—she's a bit skittish. You're so big. She's feared you might hurt her little one."

"Me?" Toddy was thrilled with being big and scary. "Me?"

"Ehyuh. You got to be still as a rabbit."

"Awright," he whispered, putting his finger to his lips.

"Jest watch. See—that old sheep, she loves her baby jest like—jest like your ma loves hers."

Toddy stuck out his bottom lip.

"Wal, you're right. She does have a new one now. But that's the way with mothers. This ewe will have another next year. And this little one will be big then—like you—running and playing on his own."

There was a grunt behind them. Jip turned to see Lucy standing nearby. She had come after all. Was he supposed to pretend not to notice? Lucy was a contrary creature. He didn't want to start her off by saying the wrong thing.

"All right, Toddy, that's one new lamb. Can you count one?"

The child nodded solemnly, sticking up an index finger.

"Good for you." Jip took his hand. "Now we'll walk quiet so's not to scare them and see if there be any more. This here one's jest fine, ain't he? We can leave him to his ma for now."

There were no more new ones that morning. The rest of the ewes seemed to be taking their own sweet time this year. Jip made a wide circle so as not to bump into Lucy and walked Toddy back to the farmhouse. It was egg-gathering time, and Jip didn't want Sheldon to think he had forgotten. He didn't want Sheldon getting jealous of the attention he was giving to the newcomers. For a long time it had been just Jip and Sheldon, and now it was Jip and Put and Jip and Toddy. Sheldon had already complained about too many Jip and somebody elses.

Jip took Toddy into his ma and began to look for Sheldon, who was nowhere to be seen. He made another circuit around the house and yard to make sure. Then he heard the squawks and protests from the henhouse. Oh, Sheldon, don't go and try to gather them eggs on your own.

He ran to the henhouse, opening the door to find a terrified Sheldon with an angry brown hen crowning his skull. She was flapping her wings and pecking at his sparse hair and pale head. In Sheldon's big hand was a smashed egg, the yellow running down through his fingers and onto his shirtfront.

"Jip! Help me!"

"Oh, Sheldon," Jip said. He reached up and lifted off the angry hen, smoothing her feathers and shushing her furious *arks* until they subsided into annoyed clucks. He placed her gently into her usual nesting box.

"Arabella don't like me," Sheldon said.

"Ah, it ain't that, Sheldon. I think you was jest too quick for her. Scairt her, that's all."

"Scairt me."

"Yeah. Works both ways, I reckon." Jip grinned up at his friend. The poor fellow was close to tears. "How 'bout you put that mess down and we clean you up?"

Sheldon looked unhappily at the smashed eggshell and the yellow goo on his hands and shirt.

"Outside—where the stink won't matter. I guess we better go wash you at the pump. Then we'll gather up the rest of these eggs."

"Will you help me, Jip?"

"Sure. You and me together, Sheldon, I promise."

Lucy was standing just outside the henhouse door. She was pretending to study the empty road as they came out, so he didn't speak to her.

5

An Infinitesimal Chance

The last frost of May had whitened the fields and gone. By five in the morning the sun had topped the eastern hills, turning Deacon Avery's distant woods and sugar bush into a dozen dancing shades of green. Bees hummed in the clover, and the smell of it, mingled in the fresh grass, was more intoxicating to Jip than a drink of strong spirits. In June the world was made new.

The time for planting had come. This year Jip was tall enough and strong enough to grasp the handles of the plow, so it was Sheldon who stood by the horse's head, urging him through the still-damp earth. Jip was full of plans. He would organize all the able-bodied and get the potatoes, corn, beans, squash, and turnips into the fields as early as possible.

In his list of able-bodied he excluded the Lymans. The mister always managed a trip away whenever hard work beckoned and the missus claimed kitchen duties. That usually left just him and Sheldon, but Put hadn't had a bad spell for weeks. He might help, and so might Lucy and Mrs. Wilkens, if he could persuade them. He eased them into it by putting Toddy to work straight off, dropping the sprouted potato eyes into the holes Jip had dug.

Lucy watched. Then she took the hoe from Jip's hands. "I can do that," she said. "It ain't hard."

"Nah," said Jip. "But it's beyond Sheldon, I fear. I'm obliged to you."

He and Sheldon ("Just you and me, Jip?") started on the corn hills. He had to keep reminding Sheldon how many seed kernels to drop into each hill. Sheldon liked the idea of counting. The actual task was a bit daunting.

At length the weather drew nearly the whole household outdoors. It was such a blue heaven of a day. Mrs. Wilkens handed the baby over to Berthie, and she began to plant the beans.

Put took over the squash, and later, when Toddy nearly fell asleep between the rows, Put and Lucy planted more potatoes. Jip and Sheldon sowed the oats. Soon all the crops were put in, and weary but satisfied, the gardeners could welcome the early summer rain when it came.

Only Jip kept working through the rainy days. He fed the chickens, milked the cow, checked the sheep. Late one afternoon, he found the last lamb, the one the oldest ewe had been carrying, lying dead and sodden, its mother bleating plaintively nearby. He got the shovel and buried it, hoping no one would ask after it, especially Toddy.

His heart heavy as his sopping clothes, he replaced the shovel and fetched the bucket for milking.

"Good evening, Jip. I may call you Jip, may I not?" The stranger was leaning against the barn door, holding a huge black umbrella over his head, blocking the entrance with his body.

"I don't know you," Jip said, his lips and throat suddenly dry, though his head and body were dripping wet.

"No, not yet." The stranger flashed a gold tooth. "But perhaps I know you."

"I got to do my chores."

The stranger moved a step sideways, bobbing the umbrella in a sort of nod. "By all means."

Jip passed the man close enough to feel the drips off the edge of the umbrella on his own head. The stranger folded it carefully and followed Jip, closing the door after himself.

In the shadowed gloom of the small barn, Jip took his stool off its peg and sidled under Bonnie's flank. Behind him, the man leaned against the timbered barn wall. Jip could feel the stranger's eyes boring into his back.

For a while—a long anxious while—the only sounds were the *plinking* of milk into the pail and the rattling of rain on the tin roof. Once the stranger cleared his throat. Jip's shoulders tensed, but the man said nothing. The pail was nearly full and the udder dry when Jip broke the silence. He couldn't stand those rabbit-pellet eyes on his shoulder blades.

"Jest what is it you want from me?"

"Want? My dear boy, what a question."

"Then how come you keep hanging 'round, poking your nose here?" He knew how rude he sounded, but he couldn't help it.

The man gave a low chuckle. "My boy, you misjudge me. I only want your good."

Jip didn't answer. He was sure the man wanted his good about as much as a hawk wants the good of a chick.

"But in order to help you—I need a little more information."

"What kind of information?" Hadn't Mrs. Lyman told him all there was to tell?

"I need to know if you might be a certain person I am seeking—have been seeking for quite some time."

Jip waited, hardly breathing. He had a sense that if he waited, the man would tell him more than he meant to. Put had said to be wary. If he was ever to take Put's advice, it was now.

The stranger continued. "A certain gentleman of my acquaintance, I might say, a warm acquaintance, even a friend—" Jip gritted his teeth to keep back his impatience "—this friend of whom I speak had the tragic misfortune to lose his only son—" The man paused. He's trying to flimflam me, Jip decided. That fake voice, like a peddler fixing to sell you something you don't want.

"This gentleman," the stranger went on, "was told that the boy was dead, but though he mourned, indeed, put up a marker, an impressive piece of marble, in the graveyard to commemorate the child—"

Jip had long since given up milking, but he didn't leave the stool. The puzzled Bonnie stamped about a bit and whipped her tail. Jip moved the bucket out of danger and patted the brown flank to tell Bonnie to move on.

The stranger came around to face Jip. He was no more than two arm's lengths away, one hand resting on his folded umbrella, as though it were a gentleman's walking stick.

He smiled down on Jip. "Yes, my boy, an impressive monument it is." Jip looked away. That smile gave him the shivering tremblies for sure. "Then, recently"—he poked at a bit of straw with the metal tip of his umbrella—"a rumor reached my friend's ears that his lost child might not be dead after all." He stopped to let the weight of these words sink in to his listener. Not a peddler, Jip thought, one of those tricksters that sell potions in the traveling medicine show.

"Imagine, if you can, our gentleman's consternation. Could it be that the son he mourned was alive?" The pause this time pulsated with the pounding rain. "How could he be sure? Perhaps fate was playing a cruel joke. Was it only a false hope that would raise his broken spirit, only to dash it into a despair far deeper and darker than even the first had been?"

Despite his resolution, something stirred in Jip's heart. It was a scene he had imagined—that sorrowing parent. He stiffened as the man continued.

"Thus, before he revealed himself to this youth, he must make utterly sure. The chance that his son was alive was so small—infinitesimal indeed—yet if there was any chance however obscure, he must pursue it to the end. And thus—" Here he flourished the umbrella, making Bonnie moo in alarm. He glanced her way, but went determinedly on. "And thus," he said grandly, "am I come."

Jip wished he had not sent Bonnie back to her stall. He longed for the protection of her warm flank between himself and this strange messenger. The thought that he might have a loving parent far away, searching for him, yearning for him—that was a daydream he'd long entertained—but for *that* parent to have sent *this* messenger . . .

Jip studied the figure before him: the narrow head with the pellet eyes, the large-brimmed hat, the tight, thin lips flashing a gold-toothed smile, the long narrow hand with almost pointed nails. It was not the figure, not the hand of an honest working man.

"Well, Jip?"

The boy shook his head. "No use," he mumbled. "I can't help you—nor him what sent you."

"I don't take your meaning."

"Meaning? Meaning I can't remember nothing before I come to this place. It's my home and is likely to remain so for some years to come."

The man lowered his head as if to search Jip's face. "And you are *satisfied* that it remain so? Even when there may be a chance"—he gave a little laugh—"however infinitesimal, that you are meant for something else, something far better"—once more he waved the point of the umbrella about him at the plank boards of the barn— "than *this*?"

Jip got to his feet and picked up the milk pail and stool. He walked deliberately to the peg and hung the stool, then started toward the now unguarded door. "Looks like I'd better be satisfied, don't it?" he said over his shoulder. "Seeings how that's the way things is." He slipped a wooden cover over the open pail, and, willing himself not to look back at the stranger again, he left the barn, carrying the milk through the rain to the safety of the kitchen.

6

All Is Well

The sheep shearers came and went. Summer had truly begun. Jip hardly had time to think about the stranger's visit, and when he did, it was with some relief that he had so easily rid himself of that sinister shadow. And yet, there was a niggling tug at the shirtsleeve of his mind. Suppose there was a chance—and the stranger had emphasized it was infinitesimal (which Jip understood to mean hardly any chance at all)—suppose, given that fleabite of a chance, Jip had been too quick to dismiss the stranger?

Jest because I didn't like the cut of the man. After all *he* ain't the lonely parent longing for his lost boy. And whatever I am or am not, I got to be somebody's lost boy. I wasn't born on the West Hill Road. I jest fell off a wagon there. Whose wagon? And *why* didn't no one come back to look for me? Wouldn't parents worthy of the name come looking? Wouldn't they, like the Good Shepherd in the Gospel, search the earth high and low until they found their lamb what was lost? I would, and my lambs is jest dumb beasts, not a human boy made in the image of God.

He should have asked the stranger straight out why it

was that this mysterious gentleman thought even infinitesimally that he, Jip, might be his lost son. Jip remembered that he had been careful not to mention the wagon to the stranger—but Mrs. Lyman was sure to have. She pure loved to tell that tale.

He tried to figure out a way to ask her about that time she'd shared tea with the stranger in the kitchen—the time she never seemed to have mentioned to the mister. Was it somehow connected to the man's popping up at the barn? It had to have been. Well, maybe she told Mr. Lyman about it later, out of Jip's hearing. Maybe she didn't want to mention it in front of the residents. Maybe.

Summer agreed with Put. Like all the plants and animals and residents, the old man was at his best in the long hours of warm sunlight. He was a great help in the farmwork, and Mrs. Wilkens and Lucy took orders from him much better than they did from Jip. Mr. Lyman, true to his nature, was seldom about when there was work to be done. If he knew the overseer was due to call, then he'd put on his old clothes and scurry out to the fields, his sleeves rolled above his elbows, yelling and ordering everyone about, even Berthie and the old ones.

Jip was too soft to make the old ones come to the fields. Besides, they grumbled more than they worked. But Mr. Lyman made a great show of their turning out to Mr. Flint, saying how *all* the residents—men, women, children, simpletons, and lunatics—all were made to bear their fair share of the load.

"Catch him once bending that fat back," Berthie mumbled as she pretended to bend her own. She waited until Mr. Lyman had led the overseer into the parlor for a mug of cider. Then she held up six beans. Jip couldn't help counting—there were exactly six in her gnarled hand when Berthie called out to him, "I'm like to faint in this sun, Jip boy. I jest cannot keep up this slavery at my age."

"All right, Berthie. Take in what you've picked to Mrs. Lyman. You can help her out in the kitchen. Hold the baby or something," though the baby was hardly content to sit on anyone's lap for long these days.

One by one the old ones, except for Put, found some excuse to leave the field. Put, Mrs. Wilkens, Lucy, Sheldon, and, of course, Jip kept on. Even Toddy dodged about pulling a bean now and again, running to Jip for praise each time.

It was shameful to think, much less say, but Jip was nearly glad that Abijah Wilkens had left his family penniless and doomed them to life on the town farm. Toddy was dearer to Jip than any of the animals, and though Mrs. Wilkens was sharpish and Lucy sullen, they hoed and weeded and picked with a will, making life much easier for Jip. The garden was larger and better this year than he and Sheldon had ever managed on their own. The result would be better eating for them all.

And Put. No one worked harder than he. At first Mr. Lyman had resisted the idea that he be let out of the cage to work in the garden and fields.

"I'll be responsible," Jip promised, knowing full well that if Put had one of his spells, four grown men could hardly handle him.

But with the summer, Put seemed so well, so unlike

the raving madman that had arrived down the muddy road three months ago. Jip dared to hope that his friend (he could hardly think of him as the lunatic now) was healed. He ventured to mention the fact.

Put shook his head. "It comes and goes, Jip. I've had my hopes before, and . . ."

"Do you know when it's coming on, Put? Or do it grab you sudden like when you ain't expecting?"

"I don't know, Jip. It seems to grab me without warning. But you might be able to tell."

"How's that?"

"I might start to say something that sounds right sensible to me—but to you is strange like. If you hear words out of my mouth that don't make full sense, you need to lock me up fast. Don't wait, you hear?"

"I won't, Put."

"Now you got to promise me—you won't wait to see if it's a passing thing. Promise, now?"

"I promise you." And on the strength of that solemn promise, he took responsibility for Put's freedom.

Toddy loved Put. He begged Put to carry him and sing and play the pipe for him. Put would sing his own and Toddy's favorite song over and over.

"Again!" Toddy would cry.

And, as though he had not already sung it half a dozen times, Old Put would stroke Toddy's fair hair and sing as sweetly as the hermit thrush of midsummer:

"What's this that steals, that steals upon my frame?
Is it death, is it death?
That soon will quench, will quench this mortal flame,

Is it death? is it death?
If this be death, I soon shall be
From ev'ry pain and sorrow free.
I shall the King of glory see,
All is well, all is well!"

Even though it was a song wholeheartedly dedicated to dying, it was somehow not a sad song. Not the way Put sang it. When he got to the line "If this be death," he'd throw back his hoary head. With his eyes fixed on the sky, he'd sing out like the sight of death was a pleasure—like a colt bolting for the spring pasture.

"More!" said Toddy. And Put always obliged.

"Weep not, my friends, my friends weep not for me,
All is well, all is well!
My sins forgiv'n, forgiv'n and I am free,
All is well, all is well!
There's not a cloud that doth arise,
To hide my Jesus from my eyes.
I soon shall mount the upper skies,
All is well, all is well!"

He sang on through "tune your harps" and "glittering crown," right on to the "blood-washed throng" and their hallelujahs. But on every verse, the words he sang most joyfully were, "All is well, all is well."

Did he really think so? Put with his lunatic mind that lay in wait like a mountain cat, ready to leap down and seize him? Put saw Jip listening and pondering.

"Don't you like Toddy's song?" he asked.

"It's a purty tune."

"Yes," said Put. "I reckon them words seems queer to you at your age. But think on me—how welcome that day—when I'm 'from ev'ry pain and sorrow free,' and 'all, all is peace and joy divine.' "

"Don't you like it down here with us, jest a little bit?"

Put reached out the hand that so often blessed Toddy's head and touched Jip's shoulder. "Of such is the kingdom of heaven," he said softly.

Jip couldn't figure what Put meant by that, but he smiled anyway. He knew it meant somehow that Put thought that he, Jip, had eased the pain and sorrow of this earth, if only a mite.

Was it Jip's fancy, or was it the way life ran, that whenever things were going well, Mr. Lyman would figure out a way to mess them up? At any rate, along about the third week of July he called Jip into the parlor.

"I've got more than enough help on the farm now, boy."

Jip waited. Was Lyman going to send him back to Slaytor's or some other cursed place? He knew the next sentence was leading to no good before it was uttered.

"But we're cash poor, boy. Nothing to show for all my work on this place. The residents will eat up the crops faster than I can grow them or pick them. And the price we got for that paltry show of wool hardly paid for the shearers. We need for someone around here to earn real cash money. Not just eat up all the profits."

Jip held himself still. He had to be that someone. Who else of all the old, weak, young, female, or simple could Lyman mean?

"Sheldon, now . . ."

Sheldon? Sheldon had to have a keeper—someone right beside him to tell him every minute what to do the next minute.

"He's strong as a mule. He can pick up a hundred-pound sheep without breathing hard."

"Yes, but—"

"I've settled it with Avery. He's agreed to take Sheldon on at the quarry. They won't pay him much at first, but when he gets the hang of it . . ."

Sheldon? Sheldon was more like to hang himself in the tangle.

"There's lots of men don't take to quarry work. Say that all that rock blasting makes their brains rattle. But that won't bother Sheldon none. He don't have enough in the upper story to rattle." The manager tapped his head, laughing at his own joke.

A chill went through Jip. He saw the huge granite rocks that must be hauled, heard the blast, and felt in his bones the thundering down of rubble when the blasting went awry. A man needed enough sense to take proper care in a place like that.

"You walk him over in the morning, soon as you're done milking. After that, he can find his own way."

"He can find the way himself anytime," Jip said quietly. "That's not my worry, sir. It's what he won't figure out after that you gotta think to, Mr. Lyman."

"Oh, he got enough sense to haul rock," Lyman said, waving Jip out of the room.

Sheldon was so proud, Jip pushed his own anxiety as far away as he could.

"I have me a lunch pail, Jip," he said. "With bread and cheese. And a apple."

"That's fine, Sheldon."

"And a water jug."

"Good, Sheldon. For when you're thirsty."

"I'm gonna earn cash money for the farm. I ain't never earned cash money before."

"I guess I ain't either. To speak of."

"You ain't?"

"Nah. I'm just a half-growed boy."

"You're a good boy."

"Sheldon . . ." How could he make him understand without scaring him? "Sheldon, you got to listen real careful to what they tell you over to the quarry."

"I will." But Sheldon wasn't paying attention. He was taking his food and the water jug out of the pail and putting them back in again, smiling at each item as he rearranged it.

"I mean it, Sheldon. Listen to me. If they say 'do this' or 'don't do that,' you got to do exactly what they say. That's dangerous work over there."

"Man's work," Sheldon said proudly, glancing down again at the shiny pail.

"Yeah. And a man don't never take his mind off what he's doing. Not at the quarry. You hear me?"

"I hear. I do what they tell me."

"Promise me, Sheldon?"

"I told you I would, Jip."

From the edge of the garden, Jip watched the dying sun turn the trees, fields, and granite trough on Avery's land to burnished gold. Milking and supper were done and still no Sheldon. Lucy and Toddy had been asleep for an hour when Jip finally spied Sheldon's bent figure coming slowly over the pasture hill. He ran to meet him. "How was it, Sheldon?"

"Man's work, Jip."

"Are you terrible tired?"

"I hurt all over, Jip."

"Wal, you been working mighty long and hard, Sheldon, and it's heavy work. If it's too much for you, I can tell Mr. Lyman and—"

"No! I want to go every day. They need me." He straightened up, as though remembering his importance. How he was the only resident able to earn cash money for them all.

So Jip kept silent. Only to Put did he voice his fears. "It worries me silly, Put. I don't think Sheldon's got the sense to be scairt."

"Well, some say it's fearsome work. Me, I like it better than farming."

"I never knew you was a stone man, Put."

"Not for long. One of my spells come upon me. They clapped irons on me and took me away. I was a danger to all, they said."

"Will Sheldon be a danger to all, you think?"

"Not to all. But perhaps to his poor young self."

Jip shivered at the words, but the days went by, and Sheldon came home every night at dusk, tired but unfailingly proud. Jip's mind loosened its grip on worry. Sheldon was doing fine. No need for Jip to cluck around him like an anxious mother hen.

* * *

Later, he couldn't remember what he actually heard and what he imagined, but forever afterward the unexpected rattle of a wagon on the road was joined with Put's voice lifted in Toddy's song:

> "Hark! hark! my Lord, my Lord and Master's voice,
> Calls away, calls away!"

It was noon. A strange time for callers. *Merciful God.* Jip ran toward the wagon. On the bench beside the driver sat Deacon Avery, silent and grim as granite. Jip raced alongside, not tall enough to see over the sides to find what in his heart he knew lay in the wagon bed.

"What is it, Mr. Avery? What're you bringing over here?" he cried.

The driver flicked his whip in annoyance and urged the horses on, leaving the boy standing in the road.

As Jip trudged back up to the house, his whole body so heavy he could scarcely make it move, Mr. Lyman came out the door and the deacon began yelling at him.

"Lyman, come here and look at what you did!"

"What is it, Mr. Avery?"

"Your idjit boy—what's left of him. It's a miracle he killed no more'n his own stupid self."

"You wanted him," Lyman answered hotly. "I wouldn't have sent him else. I could hardly spare him. One of my best hands. And you return nothing to me but a funeral expense, which, heaven help me, I will charge to your account!"

"You dare and I will make it plain to Mr. Flint that it was an idjit you sent when I asked for strong labor."

56

The argument buzzed around Jip's head like hornets on attack. He flung his arm up as though to ward off the sting of the words. Then while they still yelled, he climbed up into the wagon to look upon what was left of his friend.

Is it death, is it death?

Oh, if he could only believe that poor Sheldon was now from every pain and sorrow free, but it was hard to imagine the saints on high tuning their harps for Sheldon's entrance through the gates of pearl. Or Sheldon wearing a glittering crown singing hallelujahs with the blood-washed throng.

He threw his warm young body across the piece of canvas that covered the already cold one of his friend and sobbed as he never had in all his memory.

7

Jordan's Dark Waters

The Board of Selectmen convened and solemnly determined that Deacon Avery, not the town or the town farm, must pay for Sheldon's funeral. This meant that the residents could see Sheldon out with a proper service—not the quick graveside drop allotted most of the town farm's deceased members.

There was a great discussion as to whether Put should be allowed to attend. In the end, Mr. Lyman decreed that he must stay behind, safely padlocked in the cage, with Mrs. Lyman lurking within earshot from the kitchen.

"But I'll guarantee him," Jip protested. "He ought to be there."

"The townsfolk know him for a lunatic. They'd not credit such a guarantee."

"It's all right, Jip," Put said. "You and Toddy sing loud for me."

"You know I can't sing, Put."

"Yes, you can. There's music inside you, Jip. You just got to let it out."

They didn't sing "All Is Well" at Sheldon's funeral. Jip wished they had. He was trying so hard to cling tight to a picture of Sheldon with all those harps in heaven. Instead, they sang some doleful hymn about when "Jordan's waters encompass me 'round." It gave Jip the chills. He didn't want to think of icy waters closing over Sheldon's sweet, simple face. He wanted to think of Sheldon singing with the angels, "All is well!"

Rather than sitting in the rear of the sanctuary where they were usually relegated, the residents huddled together in a little clump in the first two rows. Jip sat next to Toddy and held his small soft hand. With his other hand, Toddy stroked Jip's arm. It was a comfort to have someone taking care for him even if that someone was a baby no more than four.

Mr. Lyman should have let Put come. There were hardly any citizens there to frighten or offend. Who but Sheldon's fellow paupers would want to mourn the short life of a poor farm simpleton? Never mind. Sheldon would be proud to have a proper funeral with hymns and prayers and even a word from Reverend Goodrich about how Jesus loved Sheldon. "Suffer the little children to come unto me," Jesus had said, and the preacher told how Sheldon in his simple mind was like a little child who had gone to Jesus and no one should grieve overmuch.

Reverend Goodrich, looking the residents right in the eyes as he spoke, gave a pretty sermon, but Jip was glad Sheldon hadn't heard it. He had been monstrous proud to be a workingman at last. That was what had killed him—not the little child part, but the wanting so hard to be a man part.

It was soon over. When Reverend Goodrich pronounced the blessing, they all stood up. Jip was the only resident there strong enough to help carry the coffin but he was too short, so Reverend Goodrich had enlisted six townsmen to hoist Sheldon's remains to their shoulders. Since the residents were all the family Sheldon had, they shuffled down the aisle right after the pallbearers. Toddy still clung to Jip's hand. Neither of them cried. Only Old Berthie cried—almost like the town was paying her to. She hadn't had any time for Sheldon when he was alive, but now she sobbed into her big handkerchief as if she'd lost her only son. Well, it was fitting that someone cry and carry on. Sheldon was due at least that.

Walking home with the able-bodied, which these days meant himself and the Wilkens family, Jip's mind flicked back and forth—from Sheldon gathering eggs and plowing to Sheldon's broken body and the mound of earth in the churchyard.

"Carry me, Jip?"

Jip hoisted the boy to his shoulders.

"Now," he commanded, "sing."

"I can't sing, Toddy. You got to ask Put for music."

"No, you. I want blood-washed frong."

Jip had heard the words so often that he knew them by heart, but they were all about death and dying, and he longed for a little rest from death.

Toddy pounded Jip's head with his fist. "Blood-washed frong!" he cried. "Sing!"

So Jip began:

"Hail, hail! all, hail, all hail! ye blood-washed throng,
Saved by grace, saved by grace!

I come to join, to join your rapturous song,
Saved by grace, saved by grace,
All, all is peace and joy divine,
And heaven and glory now are mine,
Loud hallelujahs to the Lamb,
All is well, all is well!"

Toddy chimed in on the "blood-washed frong" and shouted out the "All is well."

"Again!" he cried.

"Do you really think Sheldon is singing hallelujahs with the angels?" Lucy hadn't said a word to him all morning. Now she was looking at him, asking the very question he longed to ask himself.

"I reckon," was all he could say. Secretly he hoped that heaven would have real lambs, too. Not just the Lamb of God. He knew sheep for what they were—stubborn and stupid—but he did love them. Heaven with only the blood-washed throng and no dumb creatures would be a mighty lonesome place.

He reported all the doings of the service to Put, including Lucy's question. "Do you think Sheldon is in heaven, Put? I don't care about the harps and such—jest that he's someplace where somebody will look on him like a man. He wanted to be a full man so bad."

"All is well, Jip. That's all I know."

"I reckon that's enough."

Somehow he was not surprised when he went into the barn that night and found the stranger there waiting.

"Didn't I tell you I was satisfied with how things is?

61

Why'd you come back to pester me?" He knew he was being rude to his elders, but the man didn't follow any rules Jip knew. "Don't you have more important things than me?"

The stranger smiled, stretching his thin lips back, like a snake fixing to strike. "Oh, I'm always traveling about on important business," he said. "But I was passing through, and I figured you'd had some time to think on what I said to you."

"You was the one who said the chance was in-infini-tesimal. Even I know what that means." (He'd checked with Put to make sure.) "It means there ain't hardly no chance a-tall."

"Clever boy, aren't you?" He smiled again. "But don't you want to make sure? Absolutely sure?"

Jip got the stool and clucked at the nervous Bonnie to quiet her so he could begin milking.

"No curiosity even?"

Jip milked steadily, pretending to ignore the question.

"No? Well, a certain other party is curious. A certain very important party."

Despite all his resolution, a little thrill went down Jip's backbone. But he kept a hold on himself. He wasn't about to let the varmint take him for a sleigh ride in summer.

"He just asks I bring you to a place where he can see you for himself. If you aren't the one he's been looking for, he'll never even speak to you—but if you are . . ."

"Why don't he just come and talk to me like the gentleman you say he is? Why's he scairt to meet me face-to-face?"

"It's far more complicated than you could understand, my boy."

62

"Then it's far too complicated for me to bother with."

The man was quiet for a while, as though listening to the barn sounds—the *coos* from the rafters, the splash of the milk into the pail. From the house, Jip could hear Put's voice lifted up in singing. Toddy must have gone begging to the cage room.

"You got my leave to go—return to your important business."

But the stranger wasn't listening to Jip. He was listening to something else, his tiny eyes intent. "What's that?" he asked in a kind of a whisper.

" 'Is it death? Is it death?' " sang the sweet tenor voice.

"Oh," Jip said as casual as you please. "That's nothing. Jest our lunatic. He sings a lot."

"Your lunatic?"

"Ehyuh. We keeps him in a cage, mostly."

"He's dangerous, then?"

This was getting to be fun. "Nah. Not so long as he's in his cage. It's pretty strong. I don't think he could bust out. Me and our idjit built it. He's never broke out—yit."

The man moistened his thin lips. "I'd think," he began, trying to smile, but not quite managing, "I'd think you'd welcome a chance to leave this place."

"Oh, they counts on me here. I'm the only one what can keep the lunatic calmed down a-tall. I don't know what was to happen if I weren't here. I reckon he'd take it hard if someone was to start picking on me." Jip looked up and made himself smile right at the stranger. "You know how lunatics is," he said deliberately.

The stranger blanched. He does know, Jip realized. He's scairt to death. Not of Put, but of someone else—someone at another time and place. The man opened his

63

mouth, then closed it again. He pulled his hat down firmly before he spoke. "I'll—I'll be back, though it may be some time. Business all over the area, you know. Keeps me—haha—hopping. Meantime, you think on what I've said, my boy."

The man was stumbling over himself to get out of there. He was truly terrified. Had it been anyone else, Jip might have felt sorry for him. But not for the stranger. Jip was too relieved to have some protection against the man. He felt a little ashamed of the way he had talked about his friend, but Put wouldn't mind.

He watched the stranger's hurried retreat, humming along with Put's song. Did he have music in him like Put said? He almost believed it. Some forgotten tune lapped against the landscape of his mind like little waves in a pond disturbed by a pebble.

What a strange day. Jordan's waters washing over Sheldon. Jordan's waters. He shivered. That was the pebble that had disturbed his pond—some song about Jordan he could no longer remember.

With a sigh, he hung up his stool and left the barn. The pail was full. Even with all the distractions, Bonnie had done her best for him. Creatures was so kindly. Wouldn't God want them in heaven? They'd be so much more use to Him than the blood-washed throng strumming around on their harps.

"Who was that man?"

Jip jumped like a cat from the wood box.

"Lucy? What you doing out here?"

"I can come out if I want. It's a poor farm, not a jail."

"You jest gave me a start. That's all."

"Who was that man you was talking to in the barn?"

"I don't know."

"What do you mean, you don't know? You was talking away to him. I heard you."

"I never took you for a sneak." She bristled at that, so he hurried on. "It ain't— The truth is I don't know. He claims he might know something about me. From before."

"Oh? Don't you want to find out?"

"Yeah, sure, I do. But he strikes me 'bout as honest as a fox in a henhouse. He don't want my good—whatever it is he wants. So I told him to leave me be."

She fell in beside him, just as though they were friends, as if they were used to talking together about their problems. Jip liked the feeling. "Put got rid of him for me."

"Put? Put's in his cage, singing to Toddy."

"I know. But when Put commenced to singing, the feller turned white as death."

Lucy giggled. "He was just singing that old song Toddy begs for."

"I know. But it struck me I should kind of decorate it for him—seeing's he was already mighty anxious. I told him how it was jest our lunatic what we keep in a cage— who ain't ever busted out—yit."

She threw back her head and laughed out loud. It was music to Jip. He watched her, then said softly, "That was nice. People don't laugh much here on the farm."

"Ain't much to laugh about," she said, sobering. "I know people say my pa was a worthless drunk, but he could make me laugh."

"You ain't worthless if you can make a person laugh."

She cocked her head. "You ain't, are you?" She opened the kitchen door for him and held it. "He weren't worthless like they say."

"No," said Jip. "Sometimes I wonder at people's ignorance. They said Sheldon was an idjit boy and Put a lunatic. We know better than that and we're only children."

She smiled her thanks to him and later held the cheesecloth tight over the bowl as he poured the milk through to strain it. Lucy was going to be his friend. He felt an easing of the pain that Sheldon's death had pressed upon his heart.

8

To School

Harvest well past, Mrs. Wilkens took it in her head that Lucy should go to school. The closest common school was beyond Avery's—near to a three-mile walk, and Lucy had no interest either in that much exertion or in once again enduring the scorn of her peers. When she'd attended school in the village, she'd been known as the drunkard's daughter. She didn't figure that being a child of the poor farm would raise her status at the district school. But if Jip were to go as well . . .

So Mrs. Wilkens began to work on the manager to send Jip, too. For his own part, Jip had no leisure to waste in the pursuit of education. He'd tried before, but it hadn't been worth the chase. The building was ramshackle, the pupils unruly, and the teacher inept. He had quickly concluded, much to Mr. Lyman's relief, that learning was not for the likes of him.

But last summer between shearing and haying, the farmers in the district had built a new schoolhouse, twenty-two by twenty-eight feet, put in new outhouses, cleaned out the spring and covered it with a small springhouse, and, wonder of wonders, hired a female teacher with a college education. When Mrs. Wilkens got wind of that she was determined for Lucy to come under the influence of the only college-educated woman in the county. And if Lucy wasn't willing to go on her own, then there was nothing for it but that Jip should go, too. Besides, it would be dusk before school let out. She'd feel safer if Lucy didn't have such a long walk alone.

"We tried him at schooling," Mr. Lyman said. "He didn't take to it. Maybe he hit his head when he fell off the gypsy wagon. Leastways he don't have the mind for letters now."

"Oh, he's bright enough," Mrs. Wilkens countered. "He practically runs this place." Her eyes narrowed. "That's the problem, ain't it? Send him to school, the farm collapses."

"I run this farm, if you please, Mrs. Wilkens. It don't depend on no sniveling boy."

"Then he can go to school with my Lucy—like the law says." She was not a great lover of the law, but she didn't mind invoking it when it suited her purpose.

"If the boy ain't mentally fit—"

"Oh, the boy's fit enough. Might be the school weren't fit. I hear tell the big Brackett boys run off that no-count schoolmaster they hired last year. Some teacher what lets himself be run off by his own pupils."

"There's no textbooks to send with him—with either of them."

"So be it," she said. "We can't conjure books out of the air. The new teacher will have to figure something."

On the second Monday of November, a day so warm that the light snow of the previous day had melted by noon, Jip and Lucy set off for the new schoolhouse.

Mrs. Wilkens had been mighty pleased. She had made

Lucy a new dress, cut down from one of her own Sunday outfits. "There," she'd said, smoothing down Lucy's wide white collar. "You look fine. Won't nobody mock my girl at the new school."

Holding tight to the lunch pail he'd inherited from Sheldon, his feet lost inside Sheldon's work boots, Jip waited for Lucy's mother to finish her fussing. She was patting and smoothing Lucy's clothes like a mother cat licking up her scrawny kitten. A pang went though him. Mrs. Wilkens had a sharp tongue and a ready slap, but under it all she cared for her children. Somewhere, sometime he'd had a mother. It stood to reason. Every creature has a dam, a ewe, a cow to lick it to life and nose it fondly. But somehow he had trouble imagining himself with one. It was like he was born the day he fell off the back of that wagon. Even the stranger had failed to mention a mother—only a mysterious maybe of a father. And an infinitesimal chance even of that. He shrugged away the useless thoughts. "If we're going to go, Lucy, best we be going."

Lucy pulled loose from her mother and trailed after him across the rolling fields. "Hey," she said when his long strides took him too far ahead, "wait for me." He turned at the top of a hill to let her catch up, wriggling his toes. Mrs. Wilkens would not hear of his going to school barefoot. "My ma says it will be different at the new school, but I don't believe her."

"What you mean, different?"

"They mocked me in the village school—on account of my pa. She said wouldn't nobody mock me at the new school. But they will. They'll mock me on account of my being from the town farm."

He didn't know how to comfort her. She was probably right. The others would mock them. He could remember learning that much in school. They walked along in silence, crossing the pastures and fields going south. Ahead loomed the expansive scar in the earth that Avery called his stone quarry. It was surrounded by hills of rubble—the waste rock from the hacking and blasting of the stately granite. All this for a stone step or lintel or foundation block. As a little boy, gazing from the pasture, that distant trough of bare rock had seemed beautiful to Jip. He hadn't thought of it as a scar in the green hills. Close as he was now, he could see the gouges of the cutting tools and the blackened rock where the dynamite had blasted out the heart of the stone. It was that terrible black powder that had taken Sheldon from him. He shuddered. "Let's drop down to the road now, Lucy."

"Does it scare you? Knowing Sheldon died up here?"

He didn't answer. Perhaps it did. At any rate they swung down to the road and gave the granite trough and its little mountains of waste a wide berth. There was no one working there this morning. Avery must have his men felling wood up on the mountain. The man always had a half-dozen enterprises going. And there was less blasting lately. The selectmen had warned Avery to take care after Sheldon's death. They didn't want the quarry leaving any widows and orphans to the care of the town. A blessing Sheldon had been an idiot, leaving no dependents, they said.

The schoolhouse was a warm red ocher in the sunshine. Smoke poured from the chimney at the far end.

The yard was empty, the white door was closed. "We're late!" Lucy said. Jip licked his lips and pushed at the door. Lucy was following so close he could feel her warm breath on his neck. Suddenly the door gave way, tumbling them into the room. In the dimmer light inside, it took a minute for Jip's eyes to adjust to the scene. All he knew was that everyone was staring at them. There was a murmur of whispered laughter. He straightened as tall as he could and fixed his eyes on the front. There was a huge potbellied stove in the center. To the right of the stove was the teacher's desk. The teacher was standing behind it. She was tall for a woman and more angular than rounded. Her hair was pulled back as though she meant a stern face, but her eyes were smiling at him.

"I'd say 'come in,' but you seem to have managed that on your own. However, you could help by closing the door."

Jip reddened, much to the delight of the three large Brackett brothers sitting just to his left on the last bench. He turned quickly to obey, his mind working fast. He felt a need to master the laws inside this small kingdom. There were fewer than twenty pupils, boys on the left, girls on the right. The distance from the teacher's desk seemed to be determined by the size of the student— little ones sat on the front benches, biggest ones on the back. But all were under the watchful eye of a single ruler. For she was like a queen—no fancy dress or crown but surely in command. Her voice was low-pitched, but you could hear each word clear across the space of the room.

Jip and Lucy still hesitated in the aisle. Where should they sit? There seemed to be no vacant places on the back two rows, among the students closest to their own size. And the children on the front two rows were hardly larger than Toddy.

"Just put your lunch pails in the cupboard over there beside the chimney and then take a seat down here at the front for now," she said. "I'm still trying to sort out where everyone belongs." Teacher (for no one ever called her by any other name) soon determined that Lucy, who could read aloud a beginning primer with very little difficulty, would sit in the second row with children only a bit smaller than herself. To his immense relief, Teacher never asked Jip to read. "Why don't you sit with the Bracketts," she said quietly. "I think we need a moderating influence in that row." She handed him a book and a slate from the shelf near the cupboard. The shelf must have had several dozen books on it—more books than Jip had ever seen assembled in one spot. "And," she smiled down at him, "when the others go out at noon recess, would you wait and let me talk with you for a few minutes?"

The Brackett brothers were nearly the size of men, but their punches and snorts betrayed a nature that would have made Sheldon seem adult in comparison. They were loath to move their gangly limbs and make room for Jip, but Teacher's stare brooked no disobedience. Jip sat down beside Willie Brackett, the youngest, holding his body stiff so that it wouldn't touch him by accident.

The morning passed slowly. He stole a glance at Lucy.

She had her head bent over the slate Teacher had lent her and seemed to be working on the sums the schoolmistress had set for the older students to add. With the help of his fingers and invisible toes, Jip struggled to do the very simple ones Teacher had quietly written on his slate. Sometimes he just stared at the engravings in the primer Teacher had handed him. He tried to puzzle out the words, but he couldn't get enough of them in a row to unravel a whole sentence.

Finally, Teacher dismissed the pupils to fetch their lunch pails from the cupboard and take them out to the schoolyard. Jip got up and let the Bracketts tumble past him, then sat down again to wait. Already he knew that it was hopeless. Some of the tiny ones in the front row could not only recite their alphabet, they could make out words and whole sentences. Jip would never catch up. He would tell Teacher when the room cleared. He didn't crave the derision of the Bracketts.

"Come up to the front," she said. "And do sit down." He sat on the stool near her desk that in the old school had been reserved for dunces and disobedient pupils. There was a globe on the desk and more books.

"No one has ever told me what your proper name is."

"Jip," he said.

She waited for more.

"Just Jip. On account of some say I fell off a gypsy wagon."

"They never thought to give you a surname? A last name?"

"I'm thinking on the town record it says West—for the West Hill Road where Deacon Avery picked me up."

"I see," she said. But he could tell she thought his was a poor excuse for a name.

"Have you ever thought of giving yourself a name? A new name?"

"No, marm."

"I have a friend who gave himself a new name—Ezekial Freeman . . . Never mind. It's not up to me to tell you what to do." He was beginning to like Teacher a lot. It made him a little sad to think that this would be his last day at school. "Now to business. You haven't had much chance to come to school, have you?"

Jip shook his head. He felt like a shamed pup.

"Listen to me, Jip. You mustn't be embarrassed. It's not your fault."

"They say I ain't got the head for it—"

"Who says?" she asked sharply.

He looked up at her. Her dark eyes were flashing away. "Don't you let anyone say you don't have a head for learning!"

"But—" He needed to tell her that it was true. The sums and words just spun around when he tried to fix his mind on them.

"You're working like a man. Just how old are you, anyhow?"

"I don't know." He hung his head again.

"How could you know? You would hardly land on the West Hill Road with a baptismal certificate sewn to your bib."

Was she teasing him? He peeked a look. But there was no joking in her features. She was madder than Sheldon's hen. But not at him.

"Is there anyone on that farm who could help you if I gave you work to do at home? Someone who could help you catch up?"

"Put. Maybe Put."

"Put?"

"Putnam Nelson, our lunatic."

"The man they have in a cage up there?"

"He's plenty bright, and he don't always rave. He's got lots of good spells. Him and me are regular friends, really."

Some of her primly pulled-back hair was loose from its knot, framing her face. It made her look more gentle like. That and her smile. "How fortunate he is, how fortunate you both are, to have such a friend."

"Yes, marm. And Lucy, too. She knows her letters right smart."

"Yes, Lucy can help you." She looked at him closely. "You wouldn't mind, then, taking lessons from a girl—one younger than you?"

Why should he mind? "I'd like to be able to read and to figure."

"Good. Then you'll do fine. Just don't let anyone talk you out of coming to school now, do you understand? They're sure to try, but it's your right by law—for at least three months out of the year."

"The law says I got to go to school?" Amazing that the law should bother itself about him.

"Yes," she said. "Sometimes even the law is wise. Now"—she stood to let him know he was dismissed—"go out and eat your lunch and enjoy the fresh air. There won't be many more days like this."

He grabbed Sheldon's pail from the cupboard and ran outside into the pale November sunshine.

There was some disturbance on the far side of the schoolyard near the springhouse. He would have ignored it in favor of the chunk of bread and slice of cheese he knew to be inside his pail, but he had no sooner sat down on a stump and pried off his tin cover than he heard Lucy's voice. It was coming from the center of the ruckus, shrill and angry—and fearful.

"You leave me be, you dirty bullies. I ain't pestered you none. Leave me be!"

Jip put down his pail and ran across the yard just in time to see Willie Brackett grab Lucy's pail.

"Give it here, Brackett." Jip did his best to imitate Teacher's intimidating stare—the one that stilled the back row whenever it grew restless.

"Who'd want it?" Willie said, trying to sound careless. "Poor farm rubbish." He shoved the pail toward Lucy. With one motion she took the handle and swung it around, bashing the edge into Willie's head. The boy let out a howl like a bobcat. Lucy walked away, the crowd stepping back to make room for her.

"C'mon, Jip," she said. They walked over to the stump. Jip sat down beside his pail, still dazed by the strength of Lucy's anger. "Move over," she said. He obeyed.

Meantime, Willie's shrieks had brought Teacher to the schoolhouse door. She looked around, quickly checking the yard until she spied Willie, fingering the bump that was growing on his skull.

"Come on in, Willie," she said. "Looks as though you might need a cold compress."

Lucy watched warily as Willie stomped past her to follow Teacher into the building.

"Will she cane me, you think?" Lucy whispered.

"Why would she cane you?"

"Ma said you was never to fight on the schoolyard. At my other school—"

"I don't think this is going to be like other schools. But mind who you hit. He might swing back."

She giggled.

Teacher kept Willie on the stool near her desk, a wet rag on his head, for most of the afternoon. Then a half hour or so before dismissal, she sent Willie with his rag to his proper place and told everyone to close their books and put away their slates.

Now it's coming, Jip thought. He glanced down at Lucy. Her head was resting on her hands. He could tell she was scared. But instead of a licking or even a lecture, Teacher pulled a fat book off her desk and commenced to read. She didn't even look about to see if anyone was listening, just sank into the words like someone falling down to rest on a feather bed.

" 'Among other public buildings in a certain town,' " she began, " 'which for many reasons it will be prudent to refrain from mentioning, and to which I will assign no fictitious name, there is one anciently common to most towns, great or small: to wit, a workhouse; and in this workhouse was born; on a day and date which I need not trouble myself to repeat, inasmuch as it can be of no possible consequence to the reader, in this stage of the business at all events; the item of mortality whose name is prefixed to the head of this chapter.'—Oliver Twist."

At first Jip had trouble getting his head around the sentences—like chewing meat that's all gristle—but he let go and listened to the comforting music of Teacher's voice. It was clear how much at home she was with these words, how she loved them.

As they climbed the hill past the quarry, Jip ventured to ask Lucy about the reading.

"It don't seem regular," Lucy said. "I never heard of a teacher reading from a storybook before—a book what don't even teach us how to be good Christians."

"You wouldn't tell on her!"

She spun around as though Jip had accused her of treachery. "Of course I wouldn't. You take me for a fool?"

"That boy in the workhouse—that Oliver—"

"It was just like a poor farm, it was, only worse."

"Him being born there—"

"His poor beautiful young mother dying—"

"He didn't rightly know who he was neither."

Now Lucy snapped out of her dreamy state. "I wager he finds out," she said.

"How come?"

"That's how stories is."

"Truly?"

"I swear it," she said solemnly.

They walked along in silence for a while. Jip kicked a stone for several yards, then gave it up. If he injured Sheldon's boots, he was like to get a licking. "Maybe I could figure out . . ."

"What?"

"Figure out how to—you know, where I come from.

Without no stranger meddling between." He paused. "You think?"

"Maybe," she said. "We'll have to go every single day to find out how that Oliver does it."

"Every day," he agreed, squeezing the primer that Teacher had loaned him.

9

The Celebration

As soon as they got to the pasture that belonged to the town farm, Jip set off on a fast trot. Put. He had nearly forgotten him in all the excitement of the school day. The Lymans would have left him locked in the cage. No one dared let him out except Jip. Poor man, cooped up all day like a rabbit in a hutch. Jip grabbed the key from the cupboard and raced to unlock the padlock. By this time, Lucy had caught up with him, and the two of them led Put out into the backyard. It was past sundown, but the old man must have a chance to stretch his cramped body.

"Dark is dark is dark . . ."

Jip's blood ran cold. "What you say, Put?"

"Dark is dark . . ."

"C'mon, Put," Jip crooned. "Time to go to bed. Like you say, it's mighty dark."

What if it was too late? What if he paid no heed? The dark days of November were upon them, and Put always fared worse in the dark. He took the old man's hand and turned him toward the kitchen door. "C'mon, now, that's it."

"Dark is dark is—"

"Yeah, me, too. I don't care much for the dark, neither. Now come along, ey? You can snuggle up under your quilt, and I'll fetch you something warm for your belly. It'll make you feel better."

Put stood still as a stump. Jip struggled against a rise of panic in his chest. What if the old man refused to go in? What then?

"Here," he said, fighting to expel the anxiety from his voice, "give me your right hand. Lucy will take your left." Good girl, she took the big hand quickly, calm as though she were taking Toddy for a stroll in the fields. "Now, move your feet. That's it. Not far to go. Here, up the stoop, onto the porch. Good."

"Dark is . . ."

"Easy, easy there." Jip pulled the door open with his free hand, and somehow, miraculously, he and Lucy got Put into the kitchen, down the hall, and safely into the cage. Jip was sweating something fierce and his hands shook like palsy as he clapped the shackle into the padlock. At the click, Put's head jerked up, but he didn't cry out.

"Lucy," Jip whispered, his eyes fixed on his friend, "could you get him something warm? Milk, I think, not too hot? I'd best stay here with Put."

She nodded and ran off toward the kitchen. When she brought the steaming mug, Jip took a sip to make sure of the temperature and then handed it through the little trapdoor to Put. "Here," he said. "Lucy's brought you some nice warm milk. Ain't that nice?"

Put turned slowly toward him. Oh mercy. His eyes were like a crazed horse's. Jip backed up despite himself, as the mug was snatched from his grasp and crashed against the slats of the cage, splashing white milk and shards of brown crockery in every direction.

"Put!" Lucy screamed. "Stop that!"

Jip wanted to yell, too, but he knew it wouldn't help. Put was gone from them—at least for a while.

At first, supper forgotten, the frightened residents, with the Lymans among them, huddled in the cold hallway outside the cage room. Then Toddy began to cry, and Mrs. Wilkens took charge, herding the lot of them toward the kitchen table. Jip never went to eat nor did he hear when the others climbed the stairs to bed. The men were all asleep when he stole up to get his quilt from his cot and return to his lonely vigil.

The lunatic raged all night long, cutting himself on fragments of the shattered mug. Jip fetched a rake and stuck it between the slats, trying to clear the pieces out of the cage, but Put grabbed the handle and snapped it in two across his knee. Then he stuck a jagged, splintered end through the slats, wielding it like an ugly weapon.

Oh, Put, Jip sobbed silently, moving out of range of the broken rake handle and Put's fury. Oh, Put, don't leave me now. I need you so bad. How can I do my schooling without you?

Jip slept hardly at all that night, wrapped in his quilt in the far corner of the cage room, listening to the unearthly sounds that filled the darkness like some demon chant. He had no hope of going to school the next morning, as exhausted as he was. Put was finally asleep, but still tossing and crying out. Jip had done no chores, no schoolwork, but Mrs. Wilkens was adamant. "Jest do the milking. That cow won't have none of me.

I'll do the rest of your chores. Lucy won't go without you, seems."

"You got to come," Lucy whispered in his ear. "*You* know. We got to find out what happens."

He swiped a wet rag across his burning eyes and started out for school. As soon as he put his bottom on the back bench, his head fell down on the long desk in front, and he was dead asleep. Willie Brackett thumped the back of his head. "Teacher!" Willie yelled, "the gypsy's snoring like a old dog."

"Leave him alone, Willie," Teacher said quietly.

Jip slept through the morning. He was dimly aware that the others had gone out for lunch, but when they returned, he never lifted his head. This despite Addison, Warner, and Willie Brackett climbing noisily and clumsily over his bent back.

Somehow, though, when Teacher told everyone to put away their books and slates, he came suddenly wide awake, straining forward eagerly for the next chapter of Oliver's adventures.

Put's spell lasted until that Friday. Jip didn't try to give him another piece of crockery, but fed him bread and cheese and served him water in a wooden cup. Sometimes Put snatched the food as though he were starving. At other times he seemed not to know Jip was there—or care. His hair was wild and matted. There was food and spittle caught in his beard. The once sweet-smelling mattress reeked of urine.

It grieved Jip to see him so. And though he had no hope that anything would help, he crooned comforting words to counter the crazed ravings of the lunatic.

Sometimes he and Lucy would sing in the cage room.

" 'All is well, all is well,' " they'd sing, though everything was far from well.

Lucy, like a smaller version of Teacher, reviewed Jip on his letters and simple times tables, following him to the barn to hear him recite. But once she realized he knew the alphabet in order, she wasn't sure what to do next.

"Your name, I s'pose. Though it ain't much of a name."

"All I got," he said, then added, almost to himself, "for now." He knew how to write his name, but for Lucy's sake he pretended ignorance.

She made him practice J-I-P on the borrowed slate, and then W-E-S-T, since that was the name as Teacher had spelled it out. "You're lucky," she said. "Lucy Wilkens is much harder to spell."

"Yeah," he said. "Least mine's short," noting the difference between his seven letters and Lucy's eleven. So they decided that first he would master everyone's name. Then the Lord's Prayer—since it was posted to memorize and would be easy to follow along if you already knew the words it was made up of.

Jip sighed. "It'll be a year of Christmases before I can read a story like Teacher does."

"When Put gets better, it'll be easier," Lucy said.

Teacher helped. "When I'm working with the little ones, you listen sharp. You don't have to be sitting down front to hear."

So, by sheer stubborn determination, Jip got through the first primer. The words tricked him. He'd think he knew the proper sound, and then the letters would cheat and take on some other sound or just sit there silent.

It seemed unfair to Jip, as though words were unsteady, an undependable commodity. The little ones didn't question the fickleness of the language, but Jip did. You ought to be able to count on it more. It was ornery as some people.

Put, dear old Put, the Put he loved began after a couple of weeks to creep out from under the wild shell of madness that had clamped down on him.

He was full of remorse when he came to himself and saw the state his cage and indeed his own self was in. "The darkness seems to overpower me, Jip," he said. "I wish I could know to fight it. But I lose to it every time."

Jip wanted to say it was all right, that he understood. But it wasn't all right, and how could anyone understand the shadow that hung over his friend, ready to snatch him away with no warning, hardly.

Put—bathed, dressed in clean clothes, his hair, beard, and nails neatly trimmed—oh, this Put was a proper schoolmaster. He insisted, however, that he teach from the cage, as he felt that during the dark days of winter he couldn't be entrusted with even the freedom of the cage room. The one exception was his bath, which soothed him body and mind and gave Jip a chance to neaten up his hair and beard and nails. Jip also took apart the mattress, discarded the stinking straw, and scrubbed the cover. Mrs. Wilkens humphed and complained, but she was finally persuaded to stitch it up.

"I need spectacles, Jip," Put explained, "if I'm to help you with your lessons. They took mine away before I come here."

At first Jip was stumped. How was he to afford

spectacles for Put? He knew Mr. Lyman would refuse. Then Lucy remembered. In the cupboard where Mrs. Lyman stored the clothes left by all the residents who had died, there was a little basket of spectacles as well. Jip had some conscience about stealing anything, but Lucy had no such scruples. She brought the whole basket down, and Put tried on every pair until he found one that suited him.

"How do I look?" he asked.

"It don't matter how you look," Lucy said.

"Can you read now, Put?" Jip asked anxiously.

"Not unless you tell me how handsome they make me."

"Good earth and seas!" Lucy exclaimed. "Did you ever hear tell of such vanity?"

But Jip laughed with delight to see his friend so restored to his true self.

Toddy always wanted to come in, and though Mrs. Wilkens was obviously loath to let the little boy be close to the lunatic and listened warily from the hallway, even she didn't have the heart to keep the child entirely away from the old man he loved so much.

First Lucy, then Jip overheard Mrs. Lyman trying to persuade Mr. Lyman that the time had come to send Put to the asylum. The last episode had unnerved her, and life was always harder at the farm during the cold, bleak months. Mr. Lyman himself was seen scurrying down the cellar steps several times a day to fetch mugs of his ever more comforting cider. But if light was in short supply, money was even shorter, and Mr. Lyman pointed out that Jip liked having a pet, and as long as they kept the lunatic padlocked in his cage, he could do little harm.

"You don't call his shrieking and cursing the name of God harm, then, Mr. Lyman?" she asked.

"Jest shut your ears, Mrs. Lyman. No good Christian woman should allow herself to listen to such speech."

"And jest how is a good Christian woman supposed to shut her ears to such ungodly racket, Mr. Lyman? Will you tell me that?"

But Mr. Lyman continued on his way to his bedroom, cider mug in hand. The matter was closed. At least for the present.

Teacher was planning a celebration for the last day of school before Christmas. All the families were invited to come at two o'clock and bring refreshments to share. "Don't worry, you can be home in time for milking," she said. The students would provide the entertainment. Jip knew full well that Mrs. Lyman would not send poor farm food for rich folks to gobble down and he resigned himself to missing the celebration. Lucy, however, had a sweet voice, and Teacher had asked her to sing a verse of one of the carols alone, so she was determined not only that she and Jip should stay for the party but that her mother and Toddy should come as well. Mrs. Wilkens bullied Mrs. Lyman into letting her have enough flour and maple sugar to make a little cake. For the rest, they would content themselves with bread and cheese, and apples from the cellar.

When the day came, the snow was too deep for Toddy to walk, not being able as yet to manage snowshoes. But Mrs. Wilkens left the two little ones with Berthie and the other old ones and made her way across the fields to the schoolhouse. She had even managed to coax the loan of a lantern for the homeward trek.

The cold weather had put an end to outdoor recess. The students spent the time making decorations for the little schoolhouse. Some kindly farmer gave them a tree and greens, and Teacher had brought candles for each of the four windows. By two o'clock on the afternoon of the celebration the room twinkled and sparkled like a place of enchantment.

The small yard began to fill with sleighs from the surrounding countryside. Teacher sent the older boys out to help with the horses. With noisy cheer, the red-faced farmers and their wives and tiny babes crowded the benches and overflowed into the narrow aisle.

When Jip and the other boys came in they found that Teacher had instructed the children to sit on the floor up front. The Bracketts scowled, but one look from Teacher and they came down the aisle, elbowing one another and mumbling under their breath. She quietly sent Addison, Warner, and Willie to three separate spots on the floor, and when they had folded their long limbs and sat down, the program began.

Deacon Avery's grandson, who was the best reader, read the Christmas story from the Gospel of Luke. Some of the older girls recited poems. The little ones struggled to sing on key the simple songs that Teacher had taught them. Near the end of the hour, it was Lucy's turn. She sang in a firm, clear voice the message of the angel to the shepherds:

> " 'Fear not,' he said, for sudden dread
> Had seized their troubled mind;

'Glad tidings of great joy I bring
To you and all mankind.' "

Jip was only in the chorus, for which he was glad. He didn't crave the chance to show off in front of strangers, but he could tell how Lucy loved it. She didn't seem to care that her dress was cut down from one of Berthie's. Her chin was up and proud. Her face shone as she sang.

" 'To you, in David's town, this day,
Is born, of David's line,
The Savior, who is Christ the Lord;
And this shall be the sign:
The heavenly Babe you there shall find
To human view displayed,
All meanly wrapped in swaddling-bands,
And in a manger laid.' "

Jip was hardly listening as he joined the others to sing the final stanza. As poor and meanly wrapped as Jesus was, he was descended from a king. It was not impossible that a poor boy . . .

Jip stole a look at Mrs. Wilkens's face. There was a softening in her usually hard features. Teacher looked different, too. She had on a light blue dress and above the lace-trimmed collar, her cheeks were flushed, her eyes bright. Jip caught her glancing at the back west corner and followed the glance to see what was putting the extra color in Teacher's face. There was a tall man sitting quietly there, looking only at Teacher, as though none of the rest of them had bothered to come into the room.

Willie Brackett poked Jip in the ribs. "Teacher's got a sweetheart," he whispered under the cover of applause.

Jip's heart gave a little tweak. He shouldn't have been surprised, but still, he'd thought of Teacher as belonging to the school—to them. The idea that someone else might try to lay claim to her attentions created a little pocket of sadness in him. But he couldn't argue with Willie. No matter what happened, who was reciting or singing, the man on the back row was seeing only Teacher.

People were getting up. The children were laughing and seeking out their parents. The program was over. Outside the windows, dusk was gathering. "Please, Ma, we got to stay for the eats," Lucy was begging. She was still riding high on her triumph. People had clapped for her. Even her mother had clapped and smiled, very nearly.

"Not for long. It's dark, most." Mrs. Wilkens reached down to brush Lucy's hair out of her glowing face.

Teacher must have heard, for she came over. "Are you on foot, Mrs. Wilkens?"

Mrs. Wilkens nodded.

"We'll make sure you get a ride," she said. "Enjoy the party."

It was as though on the eighth day God had said, "Let there be food," and there was food: pumpkin and apple and squash and mince pies, plum puddings and jam tarts, gingerbread and little cakes with maple sugar frosting— and behold it was very good.

"What do you call this?" Jip kept asking Lucy as he bit into one new treat after another. She knew the names or invented them. It didn't matter. Jip ate everything. He couldn't decide which he favored most, so he had to go back and have another tart to see if he indeed preferred it to the muffin topped with currant jelly or the iced tea cake or the pumpkin pie.

"You're going to be sick," Mrs. Wilkens warned, but she didn't try to stop them from stuffing themselves.

They were the last to leave. Teacher's gentleman friend put out the fire in the stove—no school tomorrow—while the rest of them took down the decorations and the candles and stored them in a big wooden box for next year. Jip got out the broom and began to sweep pine needles off the floor.

"No, thank you anyhow, Jip," Teacher said. "Enough for tonight. It's late and by the time the holiday is over, I'll have to sweep again. Just take these branches out to the woodpile for me, please, and then Mr. Stevens will give us all a ride home."

She gave the gentleman one of her lovely smiles. Jip rushed outside with the greens. It was dark with only the faint glow of the lamp from inside the building. Willie had said "sweetheart," but Jip had resisted the idea. But that smile . . . He hurried around to the woodshed.

"Hey, boy."

Jip jumped. For a moment he was afraid, but then he recognized the shadow leaning against the building. It was the oldest Brackett.

"Addison? I thought you'd gone home—with the rest."

"I been meaning to tell you something private like, but there's never a private time in school to talk."

"What do you mean, tell me something?"

"There was a feller around town some months ago . . ."

Jip put his armload of greens down. He hoped Addison couldn't see how trembly he was.

"Wal—for some reason he's mighty interested in you. He give me cash money to keep an eye on you."

"Yeah?"

"Just letting you know. I got my eye on you, boy."

"Jip?" Teacher was calling from the doorway.

"I gotta go."

"Wal, you be good now. I don't want to have no trouble doing my job, hear?"

"I ain't going nowhere, if that's what you mean." He hurried off around the building, his stupid heart beating faster than a chick's. It was only Addison Brackett, for mercy's sake.

"Is everything all right?" Teacher asked.

"Fine," he said, "jest fine." But the words came out like panting.

10

The Caller

The three days of holiday seemed to go on forever. Having good things like school and friends and Teacher and stories caused trouble—you came to need them, to expect them as your due, to crave them when they disappeared.

Before there had been such things, Jip had been passing content from one day to the next. His hours had been filled with the animals and with his chores. He'd not much minded the quality of the food and hardly noticed, except when it was scarce. Now it was as though both his mind and his body had had a taste of a rich diet, and they longed for more. They would never again feel satisfied with the tastelessness of the old days. Life was to him now like mush without so much as a dash of salt.

If only Put could be himself—or what Jip thought of as Put's true self—the good, wise Put who sang that all was well and petted Toddy on the head and made Jip feel that he was the cleverest of boys. It was strange, maybe, but when Jip saw himself through Put's eyes, Put's unclouded eyes, he saw a different Jip. He was no longer the waif fallen off the back of a gypsy wagon that nobody even bothered to come back after. He was the boy that beasts came to without his calling or cajoling—the boy that ran the farm good as any man—the one person that Mr. Lyman and the residents could not do without.

Then, somehow, when Put went away from him into that fearsome rage or silent curtain of the densest fog, Jip himself went missing. Oh, he still did the chores, but he was again the ignorant boy who barely knew his letters—the boy that was maybe dropped on his head in the fall from the wagon and left deficient. More kin to the ignorant beasts than to upright humanity.

An ache welled up inside him. This is how it had always been for Sheldon, a continuous sadness at being less than others. The hankering to be seen as a man—that was what had cost Sheldon his life. He was not so great an idiot as some had thought. He knew the grief of being cast off as worthless, and then a few days, a tragic few days of feeling himself grown full into manhood. Oh, Sheldon, I was never good enough to you. I didn't understand.

He held tight to the slats of Put's cage. Come back to me, Put, he begged silently. But today Put lay in a stupor, his back curled away from Jip and the world.

School began, but Jip did not go. Mr. Lyman called him out of the cage room the night before to tell him he must stay on the farm.

"I can't have you going off to play whilst Put is in this state," the manager said. "It frights the women and children too greatly. You've made him your pet and now you'll jest have to care for him, or I'm forced to send him down to Brattleboro whether it takes the food from the rest of your mouths or no. You understand me, boy?"

Jip understood. There was to be no schooling for him. He should never have allowed himself to hope for it. When Lucy heard, she stamped her foot and refused to go alone.

"You got to go, Lucy. I'll never know how Oliver comes out, else. 'Sides, you can come home and teach me what you learn. Then I won't be left so far behind."

"Wal, I tell you, Teacher ain't going to like it a-tall."

"It can't be helped. We can't have Put going off to the asylum, can we? Remember how he come to us tied and . . ." But of course she couldn't remember. She hadn't been here then.

"It's the law. Teacher said so. You supposed to have at least three months' schooling a year, and you ain't hardly had one."

"Mr. Lyman'll contend I ain't fit for learning."

She snorted almost loud as a horse. "It'd take ten of Lyman's brains to make the hind part of yours," she said.

He couldn't help but smile at that. "Then you gotta help me, Lucy. Go to school for us both."

"Teacher asked after you," Lucy reported the first afternoon. "So did Addison Brackett, but I told him to mind his own affairs."

He tried not to think of Addison Brackett behind the schoolhouse in the shadow. "Did she read the book?"

"She didn't, almost. She said she hated to go on when some folks would miss out. Only you and the Turner baby was missing, and you know Teacher didn't mean that one. Tarnation! She still sucks her fingers."

He could feel the warmth of Teacher's concern glowing in his cheeks.

"But all the big ones cried out—even the Bracketts—for her to go on. 'I'll tell Jip what happens,' I said, right out loud, and she says quiet like to me, 'Then you got to listen to every word. Jip'll want to know every little thing that happens.' "

"She said that?"

"I wouldn't make it up. You're her pet, for sure." Lucy pushed out her lip in a pretense of a pout.

"No, I ain't. Teacher just knows how much I got to learn fast to catch up even to Baby Turner. It's pity for me, only. Now follow me out to the chicken house and tell me what happened."

"Wal," Lucy began, "you'll remember Oliver got caught when Dodger was stealing?"

"Yeah, yeah." He didn't need a review. How could she think he'd forget anything?

"Wal, they took him before the justice and—" She paused to pet a young rooster, who in return pecked her finger. "Ow!"

"Go on," he begged. He had to finish gathering the eggs before milking time. She told him how the kindly gentleman's heart had gone out to poor Oliver there in the dock, and how he had taken the orphan boy to live with him like an adopted son, near.

"Do you think? Nah . . ."

"Think what?"

"That the kindly gentleman might be—well, suppose he turns out to be Oliver's *real* father."

"Too old," she said. "Besides, he don't have a wife and besides . . ."

"Never mind," he said, although he did mind just a little.

And so it went each afternoon. Lucy kept him caught up as much as she could, but it wasn't the same. Not nearly. He tried as she spoke to hear Teacher's voice reading the words of the book. But it was like a tune you once heard that you could no longer recall—neither the words nor the melody—just snatches of something that made you long for the real thing.

"It ain't the same," he said sadly.

"What ain't?"

"Hearing the things that happen in place of the book words."

"I'm doing the best I can," she said. "I never said I could recite you every word."

"You're fine," he said quickly. "You're doing fine, really." He sneaked a look at her face. If she got put out, she might just stop telling him even the sketchy outline of the tale, and then where would he be?

A week passed and Put had yet to return to himself. Mr. Flint came to call and insisted on seeing the lunatic. Mr. Lyman detained the overseer in the parlor as long as possible while Jip scooted back to the cage room. He stretched an arm through the slats, doing his best to wipe Put's grizzly hair with a damp cloth, crooning to the old man as he did so.

"It's all right, Put, all right, just want to pretty you up for Mr. Flint. He's come to pay you a call, and I'm fearful he will send you off to Brattleboro, and then where would I be? You're my friend, Put, my best friend in all the world. How can I let them put you in irons and carry you off? They'd take you away, Put. They'd lock you up forever. You'd not likely sit in the sunshine ever again."

The body of his friend shuddered, but he did not turn to face Jip.

"You hear me, Put? If you don't care anything for me—and can I blame you for that? You can despise me if you will, but think to yourself, Put. You'd never sing again, locked away with nothing but lunatics to keep you company. No Toddy, Put. No Toddy in Brattleboro. Now stick your hands out and let me wipe them off. You know they need it."

There was no response. Desperation crept into the crooning voice.

"Come on, Put. We ain't got time to spare. The overseer will be stomping down the hall in his shiny leather boots any minute now. You got to least turn over and let me wipe your face and hands. Will you do that for me? For yourself? You don't want Mr. Flint to send you away from us, now do you?"

The door opened. Jip jumped back from the cage, keeping the rag behind his back as though the sight of it would somehow count against Put.

The overseer studied Put's back and then strolled around the three sides of the cage to better study the top of Put's head and the soles of his dirty bare feet. Flint took out his handkerchief and put it delicately to his nose.

"Don't you ever bathe him?"

The question was directed at Mr. Lyman, who looked confused and nodded his head toward Jip.

"You put the boy in charge?"

Mr. Lyman's eyes darted about. He wiped his hands on his trouser legs.

"I asked to do for Mr. Nelson, sir," Jip said. "Me and

Put gets along pretty good, and he's—he's"—he searched his head for the proper phrase—"like a father to me."

"A what?"

Jip's face reddened. "What I mean is, being an orphan, it makes me feel good to care special for someone. Like having family—"

Mr. Flint stiffened, his gaze again on Put's dirty back. He patted his nose. "He seems harmless enough at the moment," the overseer said at last.

Jip dared to breathe. "Yessir," he said, trying to force his lips into a smile.

"Well, carry on, then," the overseer said, giving him a jerk of the head, his large nose still protected by the gleaming linen handkerchief.

The two men slammed the door behind them.

"Rude, ain't they?" Jip said, but the back did not answer.

He tried to tell himself that it was great good luck that Mr. Flint had come when Put was in his deathlike state and not having his howling fit when he threw his body against the slats and screamed the name of the Lord in vain, calling down obscenities and the curses of the devil and all his black angels upon anyone and no one.

But at least when Put was hollering, Jip knew his friend was alive—that there was someone in that filthy shell of a body, raging against the awfulness that had taken possession of him. " 'All is well,' " Jip would sing, trying vainly to pierce the darkness.

A week passed before Teacher came to call. She presented herself at the front parlor door, which upset Mrs. Lyman no end. The door had not been opened for years and it was so warped that no amount of banging and shoving from the inside could force it ajar. The manager's wife sent Jip running around to tell whoever it was out there to come around to the main kitchen door like "any normal Christian soul."

To Jip's surprised delight it was Teacher standing there in the snow, wrapped in a warm shawl with a country woman's bonnet tied under her chin.

"Teacher?" he said.

"Jip. How are you?"

She was so beautiful, even in that homely bonnet—tall and built as strong as a brick house with eyes so lively they made you long to see whatever it was they were looking at.

"You're all right?"

"Fine," he said. He knew his face was red under the dirt. "Uh, Mrs. Lyman? She says to ask you kindly to come to the kitchen door. This here one's stuck fast."

Teacher laughed. "I've been gone from here too long. I should know better than to come to anyone's front door, shouldn't I?" She followed him around to the kitchen, lifting her skirt to keep it from dragging in the snow. "That's my pay for trying to impress people with the importance of my visit." She had a lovely laugh. Though the truth of it was, had he considered it, everything about her seemed to Jip exactly what a woman should be: see the way she stopped at the hitching post to give her horse a pat and a word before she went to the kitchen door.

"We're missing you at school," she said, as she wiped her feet carefully on the gunnysack Mrs. Lyman put out for a mat on the stoop.

"Yes, marm," he said. "I mean, I miss school, too."

"Good," she said. "I needed to be sure we were in agreement."

"I can't come back, though. Leastways not for a while."

"Why not?"

"It's Put, marm. Putnam Nelson? No one else will care for him when he's in a bad way."

"I see."

Did she? "If—if— Oh, marm, I can't let them take him to the asylum. It would kill him."

"So that's it."

"He's my friend."

She looked down at him, her eyes soft and kind. "You're a rare one, Jip," she said.

He opened the door and held it back to hide his burning face. "You best go in. It's cold as hades out here."

"Well, that's a different view of it," she said, laughing again. She gave his shoulder a little pat as she walked past him into the kitchen.

Mrs. Lyman was sitting at the kitchen table. She didn't stand up to welcome the guest, just nodded at a vacant chair. "You'd best be seeing to Mr. Nelson, Jip," she said.

For a minute he didn't move. He was hovering behind Teacher, waiting to take the shawl and bonnet, to pull out the chair, anything to keep close by. She smelled fresh as a barn filled with new-cut hay.

"Jip!"

"Huh?"

Mrs. Lyman gave a great sigh. "We've tried to make him mannerly." She gave a helpless laugh. "Can't teach a sow to sing, I reckon."

Teacher frowned but pressed her lips together.

"Boy!"

He dropped the hands he was holding out for the shawl and bonnet.

"Don't worry about my things, Jip. I'll just lay them here on this chair."

"And close the door behind you!" Mrs. Lyman ordered.

He backed awkwardly out of the kitchen. Mrs. Lyman didn't want him there. She wanted to tell Teacher that he had no head for learning, would probably be a care to the town all his life like Sheldon—being he was thrown off a gypsy wagon and never come back for.

The anger rose up inside him like soap lye bubbling up in a kettle. He could learn. He knew he could. He just had to have the chance for it. Still, how could he leave Put behind? What would they do to him? Send him off to an asylum, locked away from all that made life worth living—the sky, the mountains, the open air, and Jip, his one true friend? Lucy and Toddy, too, of course, and the animals. Put loved them as well. But it's me he counts on. Lucy and Toddy have their mother and the baby, but Put and me only have each other. We're all we got in this world. I already lost Sheldon. I can't lose Put, too.

He was never quite able to ask himself if Put, as he had been for the last two weeks, might be better off in the asylum. With all his heart he believed that only he, Jip, could care for the old man properly.

He opened the door to the cage room and went inside.

"There you are, son. I was wondering if you could heat some water. I need a bath worse than a sheep needs shearing."

"Put! Put!" he cried out. "You come back to me!"

"Have I been gone so long?"

Jip was crying. "Too long, Put, too long." He sniffled and wiped his nose across his sleeve. "I'll put the water on in jest a minute. Mrs. Lyman's got company in the kitchen right now. She won't take kindly to any interruption."

"I forget. Life goes on without me." He sounded so mournful that Jip repented his hesitation at once.

"Never mind about Mrs. Lyman, Put. I'll jest sneak in, put on the kettle, and be right back."

"I'm obliged. And," he added, "a change of clothes?"

"Yes, yes. Whatever you want, Put." The smile was like to crack his chapped face in two. "Oh, I been waiting and watching for you. Thank you for coming back to me."

He raced down the hall, stopping short of the kitchen door. He paused, wiped his palms on his trousers, and knocked gently.

"What is it?" Mrs. Lyman's voice was sharp with impatience.

He cracked the door. "Begging your pardon," he said, smiling at each woman in turn, "if I could just put the kettle on . . ."

"We've no time for tea."

"No, no, it's Put," Jip said. "He wants a wash."

He saw the anger in Mrs. Lyman's face and realized belatedly that he shouldn't have spoken of a gentleman's need for a bath in front of ladies. Teacher must think him rude.

He covered his embarrassment by grabbing the kettle and racing out to the pump with it. Mrs. Lyman was still muttering at him when he returned. He paid her no mind, poked up the fire, and put the kettle on. Put was better. Put wanted a bath. "I'll jest be taking this," he said, hoisting the copper tub over his head and maneuvering it out of the door.

"Jip—" He stopped at the sound of Teacher's voice. "We'll be looking for you next week, then, all right?"

"Yes, marm," he said from under the tub. "Yes, marm."

"That woman came calling today," Mrs. Lyman said down the length of the supper table to her husband.

"What woman?"

"She means Teacher," Lucy said, and got a look from her mother for impertinence.

"What was she doing here?" the manager asked.

"Prying into matters what ain't her concern," his wife said. "She means for the boy to return to school. Won't listen to reason. The woman argues like a politician. Ain't natural."

"Humph," the manager said.

Jip waited anxiously for the conversation to continue, but all that followed were the usual sounds of a tableful of noisy eaters chewing, swallowing, sniffling, coughing. Lucy caught his eye and sent him a knowing grin. Jip's heart gave a little leap. Teacher's won. Whether the Lymans like it or no, I'll be going back to school next week.

11

The Ghost

As the days grew longer, life grew sweeter. It was daylight now when he and Lucy started out for school, and daylight still when they returned. But hardly had a spell that would count for a real one since January.

Oliver, after many a terrible trial, was reunited with the elderly gentleman who turned out to be not Oliver's father, but his dead father's best friend. To Jip's sorrow, Oliver didn't figure it out for himself.

"He couldn't," said Lucy. "Don't you see? He was born in the plaguey poorhouse with no one to tell him nothing. T'warnt no way for him to figure it."

"I reckon not," Jip said, but he couldn't help his bitter disappointment. He'd looked to Oliver to teach him how it might be done. How an orphan boy might figure out where he come from when no one older or wiser seemed to know nor care—except, except for a menacing stranger who was making business of something that was no business of his.

The all too short school term was nearly at an end. Teacher stood up in town meeting and tried to talk the township into extending another month, but the vote went against it. Partly, it was their resentment of a woman more educated than any of them. But also, times were hard. Money was scarce. School cost money. The local citizenry were loath to spend a penny more than the law demanded. Besides, sugaring was upon them. The farmers needed their children home to fetch the sap and tend the fire and take turns standing by the boiling kettle.

The last day of school Teacher asked Jip to stay afterward. Lucy lingered at her seat, but Teacher sent her out to scrape the ice off the front step. It was just a way of getting rid of her. Lucy knew it, but she only sighed, fetched the shovel, and went out to obey.

"Jip," Teacher said when the door shut behind Lucy, "you've made great progress this term."

He mumbled a thank-you, unaccustomed to praise.

"I've wrapped a few books for you to take home. You must work on your own until school opens again in November."

"Yes, marm. I will."

"And Jip . . ." She was gathering herself up to say something hard, he could tell by the way she hesitated and then moved carefully into the rest of the sentence. "Jip, if for any reason, if anything comes up that—if you find yourself in any trouble—"

"Marm?"

"Do you remember Mr. Stevens, who drove us home after the Christmas event?"

"Yes, marm."

"Well, Mr. Stevens asked me particularly to tell you that you are to call on him—if anything, anyone tries to threaten you or—"

"I can take care of myself. The Bracketts—"

"Not the Bracketts."

"He don't mean Put? He's strange and he do have terrible spells, but he's my best friend in the world."

"I think Mr. Stevens had in mind someone else—a stranger, perhaps."

Jip was sure she saw him start. How did Mr. Stevens know about the stranger?

She was watching him closely. "The Stevens family farm is up Quaker Road on the other side of the village from you. Do you know where that is?"

He shook his head. "But don't you mind. I can take care of myself."

She started to say something more but seemed to change her mind. "Enjoy the books," she said. "I'm counting on seeing you in November now, you hear?"

"Hope so," he said.

"Good-bye then, Jip."

"Good-bye." He gave her one last look to carry him through until November, then started for the door. Lucy would be impatient.

"Jip—"

He turned at the door. Her face was full of concern. It made him want to cloud up like Toddy and cry. But he didn't. He couldn't turn back and be the baby he never was. It was too late for that.

"Jip, if you want help of any kind—and, Jip, it's not a sign of weakness to ask for help—leave a note for me at Peck's store. I pick up my mail there. All right?"

He nodded and hurried out and waited in the cold outside while Lucy replaced the shovel.

Winter lumbered into spring with the awkward gait of a moose. Sometimes just when the cold grayness of the season seemed immovable, it would disappear. Then just as you started to rejoice in the sunshine, it came thundering back. There was no sugar bush on the poor farm. Except for the few apple trees near the house, the previous owner had cut down all the trees to make way for sheep. Jip was hired out nighttimes to Deacon Avery's sugar operation—the man had more projects going than an anthill has ants. He put aside his feud with Mr. Lyman for the sake of Jip's strong young back and almost boundless energy.

Avery's sugar shack was built to protect his kettle, not the humans who sat by it. Freezing winds found every crack between the timbers. Many was the night Jip got next to no sleep, tending the fire and boiling the sap, his nostrils filled with the sticky sweet odor, the watery sap leaving white stains like strange tracks on his ragged clothes. His friends and comforters in the long, freezing nights were Avery's three dogs, who huddled close to him as though guarding their pup against the elements.

The sugaring season done, Mrs. Wilkens took it in her head (or perhaps Lucy nagged, he was never sure) to make Jip some more respectable garments. She went to the cupboard where Mrs. Lyman stored the clothing left by the residents who now moldered in their graves and found a shirt and a pair of trousers. These she boiled in lye soap within an inch of their lives, and then made Jip a well-faded but indisputably clean and respectable new outfit.

Complaints Mr. Lyman voiced about cutting down good broadcloth for a boy who was growing an inch a week were quickly shushed by Mrs. Wilkens, who pointed out that the clothes had been lying around gathering dust since before she had arrived. "When he outgrows 'em, they can go to Toddy," she said.

Jip, for his part, was mightily pleased with his new shirt and trousers. The shirt cuffs came all the way to his wrists, the trouser cuffs to his ankles, and there was a button to match every single neatly embroidered buttonhole.

"Your mother ought to take in sewing," he said to Lucy when she caught him jumping to admire himself in the wavy reflection of the kitchen mirror. "She's the cleverest person with the needle I ever did see."

"How many you seen?"

It was true, he hadn't seen many, but still, he knew good tailoring from what Berthie or, on rare occasions, Mrs. Lyman had offered him before. If he'd lost a button or suffered a torn sleeve in recent years, it had been up to him to fix it or put up with it as it was. He'd usually chosen the latter course.

He repeated his compliment to Mrs. Wilkens, and regretted it within days. For so encouraged, Mrs. Wilkens walked into town and got herself hired out to the local dressmaker. A room at the back of the shop was nearly empty, and she talked her new employer into letting her have it rent free for herself and the children.

How could he even think of losing Lucy and Toddy— or of losing Mrs. Wilkens and the baby, now crawling about and pulling herself to her feet, providing entertainment for the old folks simply by plopping down again

x

or saying "da da," which all the old men claimed as their own name? The very idea of losing the Wilkenses was as close to losing Sheldon again as he could imagine.

Lucy was no help in his distress. She bounced around with joy. "I won't be a dead drunkard's orphan or a poor farm girl; I'll be a regular somebody, don't you see, Jip?"

Jip saw. Couldn't *she* see that what she was saying was that *he* was a nobody—never had been anybody—never would be?

"Come on, sour face! Be happy for me!"

He tried to say he was. In a corner of his head he was glad for her, but the part of him that reached out to Put and the animals, the part of him so easy to tear that he tried most times to keep it hidden from people, that part of him was ripped. He was afraid to expose it anymore, lest it be torn beyond repair.

His warmth and comfort that spring was Put. With the days growing quickly longer, Put's spirits lightened. So despite the Wilkenses' departure, April and May were not too harsh. These months lacked the deep pleasure of the winter days, which had given him school and the companionship of Toddy and especially Lucy. But Put was like a new man. With the coming of June it was hard for Jip to remember the lunatic of January. They plowed the fields together and planted the crops. The garden would be smaller than last year, but then, there were fewer of them now. It was good to have hard work to do to keep mind and body busy. He tried not to think of what was gone—Sheldon and the Wilkenses—but to be happy with what he had: Put working at his side, animals being born, the apple trees in blossom, the pasture greening up, and crops breaking the soil.

He tried not to let his mind wander, because at the edge of it, something lurked. It was as though he were waiting for someone—for something to happen. It was not the feeling he had when he was waiting to know what would happen to Oliver in Teacher's book. He remembered, with a smile, hugging *that* waiting to himself every night as he dropped off to sleep. Waiting for Oliver had peppered his prayers and invaded his dreams.

This new waiting was quieter—more like a deer who knows without seeing that he's being stalked, but not who the hunter is, what direction he will come from, or exactly when the shot will ring out. None of this can the stag know. But head up, eyes alert, he must be tensed for the shot that will ring out, and be ready to spring into the air, to bound away to the safety of the deep woods.

Meantime that spring and early summer, when the work of the day was done, Jip began to read, or try to read, the books Teacher had lent him. He began with the Bible. There was a huge one on the parlor table, a gift, it said in fancy script, from the Ladies' Missionary Aid Society of the Congregational Church. But it had never occurred to Jip that the parlor Bible was something to be read, like an ordinary book. It seemed more like an ornament.

He took a look at the Bible Teacher had given him. It was smaller and more like a reading book. He tried the first page or so, but it was all in fancy words about the king, far too discouraging for him. Put explained (Put seemed to know everything) that what he was trying to read was just the introduction about how the Bible got to be written down in English and not part of the Bible itself. He should turn over to Genesis and see how God made the world. Jip did so and sure enough, he could decipher the Genesis pages tolerably well.

The second book was about Vermont history. He asked Put to read the part about Ethan Allen and the Green Mountain Boys in that. It seemed that he and Berthie had both been right. The man was part hero, part scoundrel, though Jip could tell the writer was loath to admit the scoundrel part.

The last book, and as it turned out, the one that truly caught Jip's eye, was called *Uncle Tom's Cabin or Life Among the Lowly*.

Uncle Tom was a story, like *Oliver*. Teacher must have suspected that he would work powerful hard to make his way through a story. It wasn't as fetching a story as *Oliver*—more churchy—as though every minute you were paying strict mind to the story part the writer was bound to stick in all the lessons she could while she had your attention. Now Jip was just an ignorant boy and it wasn't his business, he knew, to try to tell a writer how to write a book, but it stood to reason that if you want to catch a reader tight, the trap needs to be plain and strong with no smell of the trapper lingering on it.

But for all her preacher airs, the writer trapped him. Indeed, he was so impatient to know how the lowly of the tale would manage that he did hardly any of the reading himself. He made Put read. He wanted to get the tune of the words in his head. Listening was so much better than pounding out the sounds for himself, for he lost the sense of the story in the struggle to read it. But Put would make him wrestle with the words for a few minutes each night. He said it was for Jip's own good and Jip reckoned he was right about that.

Jip had once heard a guest preacher at the Congregational Church tell about the wicked slave masters down south. Not all the masters in this book were wicked, though. It was just that luck was not on the side of the slaves. They'd get sold down the river to where the masters and their overseers would turn out to be evil as the devil. It was a tragic tale that wrung Jip's heart for all his discomfort about how pretty it was put down on the page.

Put said he'd seen a real live slave once. "He lived on a farm not far from where I worked for some years after I come back from fighting with Old Tippecanoe. That's where my poor head got ruint, you know. Anyhow, the runaway—that's what he was, only we had no way of knowing—he lived right with the folks on the next farm and worked their fields like proper hired help. In those days there warn't a law from Washington that said slavers could come into a free state and track down men and women as though they was strayed cattle. But one day the man up and disappeared. The farmer was hurt like. He had tried to treat the man kind and pay him fair. Then months after, he got a letter from Montreal— that's in Canady, you know. Seems the fellow had gone into town on an errand and seen his old master right there on the street. He never even come back to the farm for his clothes. He just took off running and didn't stop till he crossed over the line."

"Did you ever see a slave catcher?"

"Naw," Put said. "Never saw one of them to my knowledge. Though a man like that ain't going to walk about with a sign hanging 'round his neck, scarcely. But I ain't heard of fugitives in these parts for . . ." He stopped, rubbing his big hand across his mouth, his eyes sad. Jip knew he was realizing that living in a cage at the poor farm he was not likely to hear much of the local gossip.

"Teacher said the law means if you see a slave you're bound to give him up to the slave catcher or pay a whopping fine. Only she says no true Vermonter would send another human being back to slavery."

"Your teacher's a noble woman. Not everyone would agree. But I guess you not going to see any fugitive living in peace on a Vermont farm these days, neither."

"Reckon not," Jip said. But his mind wasn't on fugitives or laws, it was on Put, whose knowledge of the world was limited by the slats of his cage—a cage he and Sheldon had built. It made him feel somehow responsible for Put's pain, though what else could they have done short of sending him to Brattleboro?

Teacher had left a letter inside this book. On the front was her name care of Peck's store. On the back a Montreal address with the name the Rev. Ezekial Freeman. Where had he heard that name before? Oh, yes. Teacher's friend. The one who had changed his name.

Though the warm, long days found Put at his best, Mr. Lyman seemed to suffer continuously from the ague, which responded only to large doses of medicinal spirits, the cider in the cellar having long before been consumed. Truth be known, Mr. Lyman's malingering meant much more freedom for Jip. It was up to him to fetch supplies from the village, and there was no one along to complain of dawdling if he and the old horse, Jack, stopped to admire a pretty view or Jip took time to eye the rows of goods in Peck's store.

On every trip he kept his ears perked for any conversation in the store or on the porch. Somedays an old man in a rocker would read parts of the newspaper aloud to the rest, and Jip would have a bit of news of the country or the world to share with Put when he returned. Put ate it up the way Sheldon would have licked up that penny candy Jip had never been quite generous enough to buy him with his one saved coin.

"Strangers in town." Jip was waiting at the counter to pay for the staples Mrs. Lyman had sent him to buy. The speaker inclined his head slightly, and Jip followed the tilt down the length of the long counter.

He had heard the old men at the farm tell tales of meeting their own ghosts. That was the only way he could explain later what had happened at that moment. As he turned his head to look down the counter, a tall, fair-headed man at the far end met his gaze—gray eyes meeting his own dark ones. He knew that face—it was the one that stared out at him every day from the wavy kitchen mirror.

12

Revelations

Both of them stood paralyzed—the man and the boy—both gaping, transfixed by the other.

"Jip?" The hateful, familiar voice came from someone standing behind the tall yellow-haired man. Jip jumped like a flushed quail at the sound. *The stranger was back.*

He dropped his goods unpaid for on the counter and raced out the open door of the store. His fingers were shaking so, he could hardly untie Jack's reins. By the time he got up on the wagon seat, he knew that the two strangers—one the mirrored reflection, the other like an old nightmare that keeps invading your dreams—that the pair of them were standing in the open doorway, staring after him as he yelled at Jack to get moving.

Poor Jack. Jip had never so much as raised his voice to him before. The old horse threw the boy a disapproving look as though ashamed that Jip had lost his manners, but he sensed the boy's fright and without further reproof picked up his hooves and rattled the wagon down the main street as fast as though he was on the open road.

Jip was sweating under his hair and out of every pore of his body. He didn't ask himself why he was so scared or why his first reaction to the sight of his own face on a strange man's body should compel him to flee, but flee he did, as though for his very life. Something inside not tamed enough to be words or even thoughts forced him on. He was already past the outskirts of the village before he realized that he was headed the wrong way. The farm was on the other side. He hadn't turned the wagon around. But he kept going north until he found himself, hardly without willing it, bouncing up the rough dirt of Quaker Road. He began then to slow, for the road was steep and no horse with a wagon behind, however urged, could take that slope at the clip Jip had been driving it.

With the slowing of the pace, his brain awoke from its stupor and began to buzz gently about as though looking for a spot to set down.

So the stranger had told the truth? Jip couldn't deny the yellow-haired man's uncanny resemblance to himself. His hair and eyes were lighter. Maybe his nose was a trifle longer? Still, all this taken into consideration, what the boy saw was his own face, even his own ears, thirty, forty years hence. He allowed himself a moment of vanity. The man was not ugly. Then he shuddered. It was as though the truth came to him on a chill wind. There was something wrong with the man Jip would someday be, something terribly wrong. He couldn't shape it into words, but the man of forty years to come was not a man Jip even wanted to know, much less become.

"If you want help of any kind . . ." His body had recalled Teacher's words, if not his mind, for he was heading straight for the Stevens farm. Quaker Road was named for him, or for his father, more likely. People talked of them because though they were Quakers, they were rich as any Congregationalist, which seemed hardly proper. Quakers were supposed to be simple, plain folk. Surely only hypocrite Quakers could own that much land and prosper so when their own sons were deserting the hill farms and moving west in waves.

Jip came to a sprawling farmhouse with attached barns, undoubtedly the Quakers' place. He reined Jack in, stopping in the road. How could he turn in at the drive? The whole flight from the village seemed suddenly too foolish for words: racing from the store like one possessed at the sight of a man who at a glance bore him some small resemblance. He should turn around at once. He should go home where he and Put would have a good laugh at his being so easily panicked. Jip had known sheep with more gumption.

"And then you turned tail and run?" Put would say.

"Ehyuh. Like a ruined hound at sight of his first fox."

Something like that. He had all but made up his mind to turn the wagon when someone called to him from near the house. She, for it was a woman, seemed old, at least the hair escaping from her bonnet was white. She wore the plain black dress of a Quaker woman, with a white apron tied under her wide bosom.

"May I help thee?" she asked as she drew close. It was a good plain face, the eyes wrinkled with concern.

"Jip. That is what they call thee, is it not?"

He nodded, though he knew no reason why she should know him. "Is Mr. Stevens about? The young one, I mean."

She smiled broadly. "I've three of those young ones

about, growing older every day. But I think thee means my Luke."

"Teacher's friend?" Jip knew no other way to distinguish Teacher's Mr. Stevens from his brothers.

"The very one. He's hereabouts somewhere. Tie the horse and come in for a cup of milk while thee waits."

Jip obeyed because he had no other plan and because she seemed so kind, and safe. The first stranger knew only that he lived at the poor farm. The two men were not likely to go looking for him elsewhere.

Mrs. Stevens sat him down in her large, warm kitchen filled with smells of meat and vegetables stewing. There was a large loom in one corner with a fat roll of finished homespun on the cloth beam. Mrs. Stevens put a saucepan on the huge iron cookstove, and when it was steaming, she poured him a cup of foaming milk into which she had stirred a teaspoon of maple syrup.

"There," she said. "It's hot, so thee must sip it slowly while I fetch Luke from the pasture. Thee will wait?"

Jip nodded his head. He hoped later that he had remembered to say a proper thanks, but he may not have. All he could recall was her kindness and his own fear—all the more sharp because it made so little sense to him. If you can put a name to fear you have some power over it. He learned that in time, but that day he was too green to have such wisdom.

He had long finished the large mug of hot, sweet milk when Luke Stevens appeared at the kitchen door. He must have run, for his broad hat was in his hand and he was breathing hard.

"Jip," he said. But he did not waste his breath on more

welcome than that. "We must get thee away from here at once."

If he had said, "We must hang thee from the nearest elm," Jip would not have been more surprised.

"Away?"

"Yes," he said. Then at the look of utter puzzlement on the boy's face, he stopped, drew up a stool next to Jip's chair, and sat down. "Thee does not know." It was not a question. It was the Quaker's realization that if, at that moment, he had broken into Arabic or Chinese, the boy would better understand what he was about.

"Oh," he said, and Jip could tell he was trying to think out what to say—how to explain. "Oh," he said again.

The impasse was broken by his mother's arrival. She immediately took note of Jip's empty mug and moved to refill it. The kindly woman then cut a slice of bread and a slab of cheese and brought these to the boy as well. She offered her son the same, but he shook his head. He was too busy figuring out what to say to Jip to be distracted with food or drink.

"Jip," he said at last. "What does thee know of thy beginnings?"

Jip swallowed the large mouthful of bread and cheese that he was chewing. The fright had not, it appeared, robbed him of his appetite. "Nothing, sir," he said. "Jest that I fell off a wagon on the West Hill Road." He didn't add that no one had thought to come back for him. He had some little pride.

"Thee does not know any more? Who else was in the wagon?"

"No, sir."

Luke watched the boy take a swallow of milk to wash

down the bread in his mouth before continuing. "Has thee heard of the railroad—the Underground Railroad?"

"Teacher give me the book to read—about Uncle Tom?" Jip watched Luke's face, still near to the fresh face of a boy with its freckles and the sweaty red hair flattened against his skull from the broad black hat. Why was the face so stern, though?

"There is no easy way to tell thee . . ." Luke looked at Jip's hands clutching the mug in one, the bread and cheese in the other, then into his eyes, as though he wanted to take the boy onto his lap.

"Thy mother—thy mother . . ." Luke backed up and began again. "Thy skin is very light . . ." Why was the man talking about his skin? Jip glanced down. His hands were grimy as usual. And in summer his hands were so much in the earth that he never bothered to try digging out the dirt from under his nails.

"Thy mother . . ." Luke began again, then turned to Mrs. Stevens. "Mother, I *would* thank thee for a mug of milk."

Mrs. Stevens brought her son the milk, and then leaned kindly toward Jip. "Any son would be proud to have such a mother," she said, smiling warmly at him before she said quietly, "Thy mother is a slave, Jip, and that makes thee, in the eyes of thy master, a slave as well. Thy skin is light because her blood is a mixture of African and white."

She paused, to let her words find their mark. But Jip did not understand. It was as though he were in a great glass cage and could see the movement of their mouths, but could not hear what was being said.

Luke took up the telling. "You were but a baby when

she began her flight, following, as many have, the North Star to freedom. Sometimes, farther south, she received help from the railroad, but by the time she reached Vermont, she no longer asked for help. She had grown confident and was traveling quite openly. Her skin and that of her child were so light, no one took her for an African." He took a long swallow of his milk, as though giving Jip leave to speak, but Jip still sat silent in his glass enclosure.

"Someone offered her a ride somewhere south of here, I don't know just where. She was glad to accept. During her long journey the child had grown larger and heavier to carry. And she could not walk to Canada at a toddler's pace." He put his cup down on the table. "The owner of the wagon—unknown to her, the owner of the wagon meant to turn her over to her pursuers." Luke put his hand on Jip's knee. "Perhaps she fell asleep in the back of the wagon. At any rate, she realized suddenly that the wagon was no longer headed north toward the border. She knew at once that she had been betrayed. When the driver slowed to take the sharp curve on the West Hill Road, she put her child down onto the road . . ."

How could Jip credit such a tale? He couldn't look into that earnest Quaker face and doubt the man's own belief in the outlandish story. But if such a thing had truly happened, why didn't whoever caught her come back at once to search for her child?

"They always told me, sir," he said as politely as he knew how, "they always told me it was a gypsy wagon I fell from. They called me Jip." That last piece of evidence, his name, would surely convince the man, in a kindly way, that this account could have nothing to do with him, Jip.

"In truth, none of us knew where thee came from," Luke said. "The gypsy wagon was someone's fanciful tale. Even we plain Yankees like a good story." He smiled wryly.

Mrs. Stevens was studying Jip's uncomprehending face. "Thee must tell the boy how we know these things, son. Else how is he to believe thee?"

"The Scriptures tell us that we must be 'wise as serpents and gentle as doves.' Those of us of the abolitionist persuasion have taken these words to heart. If our enemies are to have spies and agents to do evil, then we must employ our own covert means to do God's work. Thus when it became known that a stranger had come not once, but three times to our township in the last year, my father sent word of it through what we call our grapevine telegraph—our message route." Jip nodded, pretending to understand. "We knew of no fugitives in our midst. Why had this fellow come? We got no answer until almost Christmas."

The stranger? He must mean the stranger who'd come to the poor farm. But the story still seemed to have nothing to do with him.

Luke stopped to take a sip of his milk, and his mother, seeing his hesitation, took up the story. "Thy mother was caught and returned. But somehow she convinced her master that the babe had died along the journey."

"Why didn't—" Jip cleared his throat. "Why didn't the man with the wagon tell him different?"

"We don't know," Luke said. "Perhaps he feared to

admit he had lost thee along the way. Or perhaps he had some shame to be partner to such evil. We do not know even who he was or what became of him. When we first heard this story in December we could not understand it. There was no African child among us. Then when I met thee at the school program . . . Thee has been here for so long that no one thought . . ."

He stopped, too kind to say that poor farm residents were all but invisible to the rest of the community. He sought Jip's eyes, but the boy ducked his head. "This is a hard tale for thee to credit, I'll warrant." The man could read Jip's disbelief. He continued softly. "Thy mother is a woman brave beyond the telling. Many times, we are told, she sought to break away and come to thee. Each time she was returned."

He waited, the air full of the mother's unsaid pain. Then he went on. "A slave catcher who knew thy master sighted thee by chance in the village. We know this because a friend, one of the house slaves, was present when the slaver appeared, demanding a great reward, but the master was incredulous. For all his cruel questioning, thy mother had sworn that thee was dead. But the slaver insisted—an uncanny likeness, he said . . ." Luke paused to see if Jip had taken his meaning. But Jip was remembering the small eyes of the stranger, his mouth dripping with honeyed words. The man was a slaver, setting a trap there in the barn.

"We heard last night that this master has come with the slave catcher to see for himself . . ." He leaned close to the boy. "Has thee seen either man? Is that why thee has come to us?"

Jip didn't answer. Nor could he question further. He was benumbed, like one struck dead. The bread and cheese he had swallowed so hungrily minutes before now sat like cold stones in the pit of his belly. He put the rest of the food down on the large oak table and stared at it.

"Does thee see, my friend," Luke asked anxiously, "why thee must flee at once?"

"I can't," Jip said at last. "How could I leave Put? Whatever would he do?"

13

The Dilemma

Jip couldn't have said why he replied to Luke Stevens as he did. It wasn't, he knew, because he was such a brave and generous boy that he would place Put's welfare above his own chance for freedom. Perhaps it was because his life had suddenly tumbled over on its head—perhaps he was paralyzed by the news of his birth. He had no tools in head or heart with which to shape these revelations into meaning. He only knew that at that moment Put was all the father or mother he could remember and that to leave him would somehow be the death of them both.

Luke Stevens did not scoff at Jip's answer, nor did he seek to pry him from it. It was Luke's mother who said most gently, "But, my child, if thee stays for capture, will thy friend be better off?"

Jip had no answer for this. He hung his head to think that he was such a simpleton as to imagine the strangers would give up the chase before the fox was seized. They knew where he lived. He had no hope the Lymans would seek to hide or protect him there—the reward for capture and threat of punishment for aiding would prove too much. They would send Put away, or worse, let him die of hunger of body and spirit, locked in his filthy cage—the cage Jip had made so proudly with his own hands.

How long he sat stupefied by what seemed unsolvable questions, he never knew. But at last a whinny from Old Jack, waiting at the hitching post, broke into his thoughts. He hadn't even watered him after that crazy race, much less rubbed him down or tied him where there was grass to graze. What must faithful Jack think? He who had given his whole strength to deliver Jip from harm?

"The horse—" he began.

"Let me tend to it for thee," Luke Stevens said.

"I had him at a gallop most of the way from town, and he don't know to trot, hardly."

Luke touched Jip's arm to assure him. "Finish thy bread and cheese. Then thee can decide what must be done."

Jip tried to obey, opening his mouth and chomping down on the food, but his jaws had forgotten how to chew. It took him ages to break down a single bite and then it caught in his throat when he tried to swallow. At length he lay the food once more on the smooth oak table, mumbling an apology.

Mrs. Stevens took it up and wrapped it in a cloth. "Thee has too many burdens in thy heart, child. Later, when thy hunger returns, thee may need this."

She busied herself about the kitchen as Jip watched. So this is what a mother is, he thought. Mrs. Wilkens was the closest model he'd seen, and he knew her for a scarred and broken one. Mrs. Stevens's mind seemed busy as her hands, and he was prideful enough to wonder if it was turning over the problem of his life, just as her hands were slapping down the dough and kneading it against the table. She had large hands for a woman, but he imagined that rough and red as they were from work, the touch was gentle as her voice. How would it be to have been held in those strong arms against that wide breast?

He sensed a kind of homesickness for arms he could not remember. What would she have looked like—that mother? At least now he knew the reason he appeared on the West Hill Road. She had done it to save his life, for freedom, indeed, is life. She couldn't save herself but she had made sure that her child would not grow up a slave.

Would she sorrow to know that those years of freedom had been spent on a poor farm? Would it sadden her to think that Jip had no family but the town to protect him and no name but the one called forth by the peculiar circumstances that added him to the town's roll of paupers? Some might think a poor farm little better than bondage. But Jip knew better. He had, as Father Adam in the Bible, dominion over the animals in his little Eden. Nor was he lonely as Adam in the garden—he'd had Sheldon and Lucy and Toddy and the rich if painful friendship with Put. Teacher, he knew, cared for him, and now the Stevenses did as well.

If Luke Stevens had ways to get word from the South, then perhaps he could send a message to that grieving mother that she had done right to throw her baby child off the wagon, that her son was rich and free, learning day by day to read and write and figure. She'd be so proud she bore him that she could cast off the shame of how he had been conceived.

Because boy though he was, Jip knew as well as any man what had been done to her. She would not have fled if she had chosen freely to bear her master's child.

It is hard to say if all these thoughts went through Jip's head during the space of time while he waited for Luke Stevens to return or whether they came in pieces later, but when Luke returned, the boy was no nearer to decision than when the man had left.

Perhaps that is why he blurted out so ill conceived a plan that it was bound to miscarry.

"I will flee, as you say," he said. "But I must take Put with me when I go."

The Stevenses, mother and son, passed a look but not a word between them. Luke sat down again on the stool beside Jip and asked with the earnestness of a boy questioning a man: "How will thee accomplish this, Jip?"

Jip had no answer, but he pretended to ponder, thinking out a plan even as he spoke. "We will leave tonight," he said. "If I jest follow the North Star like you said . . ."

"We can help thee," Luke said quietly. "There are friends all along the way northward. We call them stations on our secret railway."

"Then it will be easy," the boy said. "Jest tell me the way."

"I can tell thee one station only," Luke said. "We have found it is safer not to carry too much knowledge."

"Safer?"

"For others," he said. "Sometimes—sometimes, under painful questioning, a person tells what he would not otherwise."

"I'd never betray—" he began and then stopped. Who knew what one might do? To play the man might cost others their lives and hopes. "What's the first station, then?"

"Thee is sitting in it." Mrs. Stevens lifted her floury hands and slapped the dough against the tabletop.

"I'll bring him here tonight," Jip said, "if you will help us on."

Luke stood up, ready to see Jip out. "With God's help, we will see thee both safely on," he said.

Jip untied the horse and climbed into the wagon, not worried so much about the flight as the explanation he must concoct for his long absence from the farm, his winded horse, and his empty shopping basket. His mind elsewhere, he took the food Mrs. Stevens had given him from his pocket and chewed nervously at it, until, to his unhappy surprise, it was gone.

And, as it turned out, he needn't have worried about an explanation. Mr. Lyman's ague was most severe, and he was keeping Mrs. Lyman running back and forth to fetch him relieving medication and between times demanding her attention for his noisy complaints.

Jip led Jack into his stall, rewarding him with a handful of oats as well as a manger of hay, and went directly to milk. When he brought in the pail there was no evidence of supper preparation, so he stoked up the stove, put on a pot of water to boil, and made mush for everyone. After he got the others to the table, he took his own bowl and Put's back to the cage room.

Put was sitting cross-legged in the corner of the cage like a Chinese scholar, his spectacles halfway down his nose, reading Teacher's Bible.

Jip put down the bowls, then, making sure the hallway was clear, closed the door and came close to the cage.

"Hallo, Jip," Put said. He seemed in the brightest of spirits, for which Jip gave fervent, if silent, thanks to the Almighty. "You needn't tiptoe about. The manager's been like a wild brute in bedlam all day. But I thank you for closing the door. Now I can read in peace."

"Put." Jip's mouth was at the slats and he was whispering, which caused the old man to put down his book, remove his spectacles, and study the boy's face as if Jip were the odd one.

"Put," he repeated. "It's too long a tale to tell you now, but the stranger is back and this time they mean to kidnap me."

"Kidnap?"

"Shhh. I know it sounds crazy, but it's full truth. So—"

"So?"

"So I got to run."

"Run?" Now the old man had come close to the bars and was whispering as well. "Why? How? Where would you go?"

"We."

"What do you mean?"

"We. You and me. That is, if you're game to make a run for the border."

Put cocked his head. "Canady?" he asked.

Jip nodded. "There's them what will help us—if you be willing. I won't go without your coming, too."

He set the spectacles back on his nose as though Jip were a book in such small print he couldn't read it else. "Why are you so set on Canady?"

"You remember," Jip cleared his throat. "We was talking about it jest days ago. That law from Washington about runaway slaves . . ."

"You didn't run away, boy. You fell off a wagon."

"Seems I was kinda pushed by—my—my mother. She was fleeing them and about to be caught up to, there on the West Hill Road."

Put's mouth dropped open and Jip found himself studying the poor old red gums and missing and decayed teeth. Put closed his mouth, removed his spectacles, and, folding them carefully, set them on his knee. "I won't be going with you," he said. "I'd only hold you back. You know that, son. What you need is speed—to move fast and invisible. Take me along and it'll be like trying to run with a millstone hung 'round your neck."

"Then I won't go neither."

They were both quiet, each searching the other's face for a sign of weakness, a hint that one would give in to the other's demand. Put looked away first.

"If you stay here, they'll catch you. No mistake about it."

"I'll take my chance."

"That's no chance, boy. It's certain as death."

"Then so be it."

He sighed so deeply that Jip knew he had won.

"When do we leave?" the old man asked.

"Tonight." He could hardly keep the excitement from creeping into his voice. "Tonight. Soon as they're all asleep."

14

Taking Flight

Jip told Old George that he would be sleeping in Put's room that night. As he often did this to keep the lunatic calm, no one would think it strange. Nor did he worry about provisions. It was only a few miles north to the Stevens farm, and he knew he could count on the Quakers to more than supply them with what they needed for the next stage of the journey. He had a bit of pride about taking from the farm's store of food. He didn't want anyone, after he was gone, to remember him as a thief.

There was enough moon for the travelers to see their way as they crept out of the house and across the yard. Jip spared a pang of conscience for the beasts. Who would milk Bonnie in the morning or take Jack out to pasture? And no one would pay those poor stupid sheep any mind at all. But he knew in his heart that there was no help for what he was doing. He was getting away and Put was coming with him. Thank the Lord. He hadn't much fancied sitting around like a prize pumpkin waiting to be plucked.

Where were the strangers sleeping this night? Indeed if they slept at all. How did such men go about the business of tracking and trapping other human beings?

Except for what he had read in Mrs. Stowe's book, he knew so little of it all. He had not realized until yesterday that there were folks close by who were set to disrupt this murderous pursuit. Perhaps Teacher had given him that book on purpose, as a warning, so he would know that he mustn't let himself be caught.

He had to be careful of his pace. They were both barefoot, but Put's feet, too long indoors, were tender and he stepped almost daintily on the rough ground. *If he sees he's holding me back, he'll refuse to go on. I got to watch it. I can't waste precious time arguing whether to move forward or back.*

They would be most exposed during the early part of the trip. Jip wasn't expecting the slavers to be out, but how could he be sure? For the first hour or so they followed the road. The early August moon lit their path. Put stopped to point out the Big Dipper and the North Star the fugitives were said to follow. Jip tried not to be impatient. Perhaps they should have cut across the fields, but that would have meant climbing stone walls and rail fences, moving up and down across the rocky ground. Nor would they be better hidden. Someone's dog was like to set up a bark, causing them to be shot as marauding foxes or thieves. And there was no cover to hide behind in those pastures. Most had been cut for potash years before and kept clear by grazing sheep.

They did go east through pastureland to bypass the village, and then it occurred to Jip that at the rate they were walking it would be daylight long before they reached the Stevenses. Put, so out of practice walking, had to stop and catch his breath at every little hill. Jip decided it would be better not to follow the road any longer but to cut up through the woods and hit Quaker Road at an angle, not far from the Stevenses' farm. He didn't discuss his plan with Put. The old man was tired and looked to be feeling every stone and twig underfoot.

The boy had a fair notion of direction in the daytime. Like anyone who works outdoors, he knew where the sun lay at various times of the year and at different hours of the day. He could not recollect ever being lost in daylight. But he had not reckoned for the night. He did not know his way, as sailors do, by the stars, though knowing how the Dipper pointed helped. Once in the woods, however, with no stars in view and hardly any light of the moon shining through, they might as well have been blindfolded. He could only crash forward. Put was probably trying as hard not to ask if Jip knew the way as Jip was trying not to say how very lost they were.

The way—which was what Jip had to call it even though it was just the direction his feet were taking him—went uphill so steeply that he could hear Put behind him panting. The old man was grabbing branches to pull himself forward, letting each one go with a crash as he reached out to grasp the next. A pair of bucks fighting for a doe would have been quieter. But how could Jip scold Put for trying to keep up on a journey he'd forced him to take? As soon as they reached a level spot, Jip stopped. When Put was beside him, the boy dropped all pretense. "I ain't got the smallest notion of where we are, Put. We might as well find a spot and settle down till morning."

The old man mumbled something Jip took to be

assent. It seemed clear he was too tired to speak. They huddled together for warmth against the broad trunk of a tree. "Best try to sleep," Jip said.

Put may have slept a little. His panting ceased and his breath came more regularly. Jip could have sworn that he never closed his own eyes, but he must have, because suddenly the bright sun of a summer morning penetrated the leafy ceiling of the woods. Jip looked at Put. His eyes were open, though bloodshot and very weary.

His own limbs were stiff, but the boy struggled to his feet, stretched, then reached down to help the old man up. Put tried to make a joke of it. How after all that time sleeping in the luxury of his cage had spoiled his bones. They had plumb forgot how to rough it in the open. Why, when he'd been in the army back in '12, '14, many's the night . . .

At last Jip had him on his feet. "Lead on!" Put said. The tone of fake cheer in his voice made Jip want to cry. If he could get a good glimpse of the sun and take his bearings, he was sure he could lead them to Quaker Road. He hoped he was right—that Quaker Road wound up the far side of the hill on which they stood. "Well, Put," he said at last. "Let's try it this away."

They walked. Jip forced himself to take the pace at nearly a crawl. Finally he figured they must be near the road, if not yet parallel to the Stevenses' farm. They came upon a stream that must be forded. The water was lively and swift, but this late in the summer less than a foot in depth.

"Here, let me give you a hand," Jip said, stepping into the cool water. "These rocks are a mite slippery."

The old man waved him off. "You go on ahead," he said. "Scout it out. Like we used to do in the war. Find us the best route. I'll jest wait here. Get a bit of a rest."

Jip didn't want to go on without him, but he doubted that he could sling the old man over his back and carry him. So he left him there. At least there was water in the stream, even though Put'd have to bend down and lap it like a dog. In all his pride Jip had not even provisioned the two of them with a tin cup for their great journey. For the hundredth time he repented his mindless eating of Mrs. Stevens's bread and cheese.

"I'll be back afore you know it," he promised.

Without Put to slow him down, Jip could move fast as a hare through the brush, and in what seemed to him no time at all, he spied through the trees the winding ribbon of packed earth that must be Quaker Road. He hadn't altogether gotten them lost, or indeed led them far astray of their goal. He allowed himself a moment of pride over that. Then, keeping well under the cover of the trees, he followed the road as it wound farther uphill until, at last, he spied the great red barn and sprawl of white frame buildings that made up Quaker Stevens's homeplace.

Smoke was pouring from the chimney. The boy fancied he caught the smell of corn mush and griddle cakes cooking on the black iron stove. He could have sung out with joy. He would present himself at the door and ask for help bringing Put in from the woods.

He had left the trees and started across the road when a sound came to his ears—the rattle of a carriage and the pounding of hooves on the hard-packed dirt of the road.

He wasn't frightened, but caution sent him back into the trees to let the traffic pass. He knew he shouldn't let himself be seen.

He recognized the horse at once. He knew most horses in the county by sight. It was one from the village livery stable, and it struck him as strange that someone would be out in a hired carriage at this hour of the morning. The lack of sleep must have made him dull. He didn't recognize the driver or the passenger in their top hats and well-cut suits. He was surprised when the carriage failed to continue up the road but turned into the Stevenses' drive and stopped. The driver tied the horse to the same post where Jip had hitched Jack only yesterday. Then the passenger stepped down and the two of them went to the door.

The one who was the driver pounded on the door. Rude, thought Jip. I'd of thought such gentlemen had more manners. An older man, Quaker Stevens himself most likely, answered the door. Jip could not hear his gentle greeting, but his own heart jumped into his mouth as the driver began to wave something in the Quaker's face and a hatefully familiar voice cried out, "Give him up at once! We have a warrant!"

Quaker Stevens did not move, but the driver pushed him roughly aside and the two strangers strode past him into the farmhouse.

15

Hunted

Jip's heart was pounding like summer thunder against his chest. What could they do? He, perhaps, could make his way to the border some whichaway. It couldn't be more than a two-week walk, but what of Put? He had counted on the Quakers to find transport for them. He hadn't thought that Put would need to walk it. What had he done bringing Put along? Would a cell in an asylum be worse than death from hunger or exhaustion in the wild? He must go back at once to where Put waited, confess his selfishness and stupidity, and take his friend back to the poor farm.

For what? Death from despair and neglect? He shivered, then sat down on the floor of the woods, unable to go forward or back. I'll watch the house, he reasoned. When they find I'm not there, they'll leave and go hunt for me elsewhere. They're not so clever. Else they'd have come to the farm last night. He began to sweat. Suppose they had? He'd taken a dreadful risk going back there. Why had they not gone there last night? Why, instead, come here so early in the day? They had wind of the Stevenses, that was it; they suspected them of aiding fugitives.

The slavers must surely have searched every inch of

the house, the outbuildings, and the barn. Or it seemed they had. He sat so long and so still there on the leaves and litter of the forest floor that a little vanguard of ants hurried over the mountain of his bare foot and came back sometime later, lugging a beetle many times their size. Jip watched the little creatures, tugging and pulling and pushing their feast. He almost reached down and lifted the beetle across his foot for them, but he stopped himself. There was something comforting about that kind of grit. It was like a message. The ants were telling him that he mustn't lose heart so easily.

The slavers were out of Jip's sight for near eternity, until at last his straining eyes saw them come out of the barn door, accompanied by a small troop of male Stevenses.

They were too far away for Jip to hear what was being said, but from the gestures of the driver, it was clear that he was furious not to have found his quarry. The other— Jip could not call him master, much less . . . The other stood stiffly by. As far as Jip could tell, the pale man said nothing. At length they left the Stevenses and returned to their hired carriage.

As they turned out of the drive and into the road, Jip could catch bits of their conversation, for the angry driver spoke louder than a gentleman ought. The pale man had apparently proposed that the driver stay behind to watch the house, while he himself returned for his breakfast at the tavern.

The driver, the person that Jip had long thought of as the stranger, but whom he now knew to be a slave catcher, was vocal in his displeasure at the idea. Was he then to be left on a country road with no horse and no provisions, not even a stool upon which to sit? He also made some half-joking remark about the large-sized, unfriendly Friends, betraying a certain nervousness about the Stevenses' household.

The pale man was not sympathetic. His voice was much lower, and Jip caught only the words "yonder woods" as the man tossed his head in Jip's direction. The boy didn't wait to hear more, but slipped away through the trees at once. At least they had no hounds. In the book Teacher had given him, the slavers ran a pack of bloodhounds.

He found Put near the spot where he had left him, though during his long wait, the old man had moved to get himself a drink of water. He had heard the boy coming and was looking up with so much expectation in his old tired face that Jip could hardly bear to tell him the news.

"So," Put said when he heard, "that cursed feller is keeping a watch on the house."

"Yes." How could he soften it? "You figure he's got to eat or sleep sometime," knowing as he said it what cold comfort the words offered.

"Appears to me," Put said, his mouth twisted into an attempt at a smile. "Appears to me, you and me is in a pickle barrel without a fork."

Jip gave a weak laugh. "If only I had brought us food."

"And quilts."

"And a jug of cider."

"And a pouch of tabaccy."

"You don't smoke, Put."

"I was thinking of taking it up, with so much time on my hands."

Who could have guessed that Old Put could get him

laughing—and them in such dire straits? For the first time in hours, Jip felt something like happiness that he had brought his friend along. Though he sobered quickly. He knew their laughter couldn't be heard as far as the road, but they must get into the habit of caution. It didn't come naturally to either of them.

"We got to put our brains to it, Put. I think they're like to give us up in a day or two, but meantime, we got to get off this damp ground and get something into our hollow bellies."

"There's huckleberries over in that clearing near the stream," he said. "I spied them when I was getting a drink."

"Huckleberries is fine," Jip said. "I always fancy them this time of year, don't you?" But the few he found were dried and not too tasty. They both made a show of enjoying the scarce handful. Then Jip took a long drink from the stream to give himself time to think out what they must do next.

Put had been thinking as well. "You're right, you know. The feller can't stay there forever, and I've got a good notion that the other pretty gentleman"—said in a voice to make Jip understand that he could not truly consider a slave owner a gentleman—"will feel himself too proud to take a turn at sentry duty."

"So?"

"So they can't capture you, not legal like, without the sheriff or some such officer of the law . . ."

"Ey?" He hadn't known that. Maybe Put did have an idea that might help.

"You go back there"—he raised his hand to keep Jip from interrupting—"*alone*. Two is two to make noise in the bush. You go there and watch the watcher. When he leaves, for he's going to have to leave sometime, you hightail it to the house. They'll have a place to hide you, won't they?"

"But—"

"You can send someone back for me. Even if they was to stumble acrost me here, they're not likely to trouble themselves to arrest a lunatic. And if they do, they'll just throw me into a cage. And a cage, my boy, is home sweet home to me."

He didn't like Put's plan. It meant leaving his friend alone again, but Jip didn't have another plan to offer. He took off his outer shirt and folded it as a kind of pillow for Put to sit on. Though Put gave a show of protest, he settled his old bones on it, leaning against the sugar maple tree that the two of them had begun to think of as their own—as close as they had to a refuge in the woods.

When Jip started once more for Quaker Road he was conscious of every twig cracking under the soles of his feet, the cry of every startled bird, or scurry of chipmunk, the slightest rustle of the branches he brushed past. He must get close enough to keep the slave catcher in sight without arousing the slightest suspicion in the man that he was being watched.

Perhaps he should climb a tree and hide himself among the branches. Then he could look down upon the whole scene, keeping the sentry in sight as well as the farmhouse and whatever traffic might be coming up the road. The trick was to climb making no more noise than a squirrel. The slave catcher was an edgy sort of fellow. Anything was likely to fright him. See—he had pulled his watch out of his pocket once again. Now he was peering down the road. He was on his feet. Jip froze. But, as he suspected, the man's jerky behavior was just nervousness. Look-a-there. The man couldn't seem to sit still. Down under all that bluster, the man was shaky as an aspen in a windstorm. The slaver tried pacing a bit, as much as one could confined by the trees and hidden from the road. He looked this way and that. Once Jip thought the man might have looked straight at him, but if he had, he'd seen nothing, for he took a step or two in the opposite direction before coming back to sit down again on his fallen log.

Jip crept a few feet deeper into the woods, looking for a tree tall and full enough to suit his need. He spotted a tall beech. He had hardly shinnied up its smooth, gray trunk to a low fork in the branches than he heard the sound of the horse and carriage on the road. A squirrel scolded and birds flew up squawking as he climbed, but he could only hope that the noise of the traffic would cover his scramble. Thirty, maybe forty feet up, he sat himself on a strong limb, holding tightly to the trunk. He had chosen well. His perch lifted him above the canopy of the woods. A good stretch of the road was in sight.

The pale stranger's carriage was followed by someone on horseback. Who was it? Yes, the sheriff had come this time. When they got to the spot where the slave catcher had hidden himself, he stepped out into the road. The carriage and horseman stopped. There was a consultation. Sheriff Glover seemed annoyed. At length, and after extended discussion, the slave catcher climbed up into the carriage. The pale man backed and turned the horse.

Soon they would be returning to the village. Jip waited for them all to move on, but they went no farther. What were they waiting for? All three of them were looking down the road. There was annoyance in the way they held their bodies; even the horses stomped and flicked their tails impatiently.

At long last a single clumsy horse came plodding up the hill, two men on its broad back. Jip recognized the horse before he recognized the riders. It was the Bracketts' much abused plowhorse with Addison and Warner astride.

Judging by the gestures, the slave catcher and the brothers were having a heated exchange. Addison was the talker. Warner just sat there, wiping his face on his sleeve. At length they dismounted. They seemed to be tying the horse, though Jip couldn't be sure. After a few more words, the pale man flicked the reins and the carriage started down the road followed by the sheriff. Jip could no longer see the Bracketts, only the rear end of their horse, his tail sweeping his broad rump. Maybe the brothers had sat themselves down on the slaver's fallen log. But it was clear: They were here to watch that no one entered the farmhouse.

What was he to do? The Bracketts had no love for him. They probably thought stalking a fugitive great sport—and one that put money in the pocket besides.

If he had been less tired, if his belly had been less hollow, he would have seen what to do much earlier. There must be a door to the farmhouse on the pasture side. If he made his way up beyond the next bend of the road, he could cross over, steal down the fields and pasture, and come in from the west side of the house. The land was cleared, but it was hilly. There was a good chance he could make it without the Bracketts seeing him. He didn't give the boys much credit for common sense—or vigilance either, for that matter.

He slid down the beech tree, taking care to land softly on the leaf-strewn ground, grateful the Bracketts hadn't thought to bring their dogs along. His heart was pounding so loud that it was a wonder the boys couldn't hear it. He crept several hundred feet north, well beyond the next curve of Quaker Road.

He raced across the fields, not even daring to check that no one was watching. His goal was a huge wooden watering trough, the only hiding place he could spot in the pasture. The cows coming to and from the trough eyed him with considerable suspicion as he squatted there. He held still for several minutes, both to catch his breath and to let the cows become accustomed to his presence. Then he got to his knees and slowly raised his head, his eyes just above the level of the trough.

The farmhouse complex blocked any view of the Bracketts or their horse. Jip spoke gently to the cows. He couldn't risk upsetting them. It would send an alarm even to the thick heads across the road if they saw a bunch of cattle suddenly dancing out from behind the barn. I can make it easy if I move slow and quiet and don't scare the cows, he thought. He had hardly taken his first cautious step when suddenly, sending his stomach bolting into his gullet, a big hand reached across his shoulder and clamped down on his open mouth.

16

The Cabin

"Jip. I did not mean to frighten thee, but thee must not go to the house. They are watching it."

"Just the Brackett boys," Jip whispered. He knew, if Luke Stevens didn't, that those fellows had less gumption than a lovesick moose.

Luke put up a finger to shush conversation, turned Jip about, and headed him right back the way he'd come. "Stay low," he muttered under his breath. He paused a minute to pump some water into the trough and then began a casual saunter among the cattle, motioning to Jip to stay behind the bodies of the beasts while he stooped now and again to inspect an udder or look at a backside. In this way the two of them made their way northward across the pasture to the curve of the road and into the woods on the other side. In the safety of the trees, he explained.

"We know there are others just down the way. There may be more elsewhere. They hope to trap thee into coming into the house. There's a cabin farther up—at the end of the road. I think thee will be safe there until nightfall. Then, if all goes well, we can convey thee to the next station."

"Put—I left Put . . ."

"Where has thee left him? Tell me and I'll fetch him here. It is not safe for thee to be abroad."

Jip described the place as best he could. Luke knew the spot. The woods were on their land, he said, and he had hunted in them the better part of his life. Jip was not to worry. They were walking as they spoke, keeping to the protection of the trees until, finally, the cabin came into sight—a rough log one-room structure—the kind built in the olden days or even more lately by those too poor to raise a proper clapboard house. Still, weatherworn as the logs were, the roof was newly shingled and the small windows sported glass panes.

Without knocking, Luke lifted the latch and pushed open the door for Jip to enter. There was no fire on the hearth and no sign about of the cabin's residents.

"I think thee should stay in the loft," Luke said. "If by chance someone should peer in the window—though no one has come looking here as yet. I'll bring thee food as soon as I am able. Meantime"—he reached into a crock and took out a handful of hard biscuits—"this is the best I can offer." He grinned. "My mother would be mortified to treat a guest so. Now climb up and I will serve thee thy breakfast."

All Jip could think of was Put. He'd make himself sick trying to eat those berries. Oh, why hadn't he saved the bread and cheese for him? "When you go to find Put, he'll be powerful hungry."

"Don't be anxious. I'll see him to better than this, I promise."

Jip climbed up the ladder, then reached down for the

biscuits and a cup of water Luke had dipped out from a bucket near the sink. The Quaker bade a quick good-bye then and closed the door after him. He was outside for a while, stacking something—was it firewood?—against the door. Not to keep him in, Jip guessed, but to try to keep his enemies out.

He ate the hardtack biscuits hungrily, washing them down with water, and fell back on the mattress to sleep like one dead. He awoke once to hear the sound of rain on the roof, but Put was safe, Luke had promised, so he turned over and slept again. The next sound he was conscious of was a noise at the back of the cabin—that of a window being raised. He peered through the darkness without daring to breathe. A dark round form clanked against the plank floor. Then one long leg followed another across the sill, until the whole of Luke Stevens's body slipped into the cabin.

"Jip," he called softly. Even when there was no immediate danger the man had the habit of quiet.

Jip leaned over the edge of the loft. "Where's Put?"

"He's with my mother. He needs more care right now than either thee or I can give him."

"He's not—"

"No, he has not left his senses, but he is cold and hungry. Providence is testing us with a bitter rain tonight, and thy friend got the worst of it. Even the sentries seem to have left off watching."

"Can I come down, then?"

"Yes and I'll make a fire as well. Unless . . ." He hesitated. "Jip, thy friend will not be traveling tonight. He said for thee to go on ahead. That he would follow."

"I can't do that," Jip said.

Luke sighed. "I said as much to him." He had the fire going quickly and hung above it the kettle he had brought. On top of the kettle lid he laid slabs of bread to warm. The smell of bubbling meat and vegetables and the steaming bread was as close to heaven as any boy of a poor farm is likely to get this side of the grave. Luke watched him eat, refusing to join him. "If I take rations my mother has sent for thee, she'll take her broad hand to my hide, woman of peace though she claims to be," he said.

With the last hunk of bread Jip was sopping up every drop of the rich gravy that clung to the sides and bottom of the kettle when Luke began to speak. "We do not know what the slavers intend—beyond their certain intention to recapture thee alive. They will not want to hurt thee, for that lessens thy value to them. But they have many tricks and they have been diligent in this hateful business for so long that we on the other side must be, as I said, wise as serpents when we try to match wits with theirs."

Jip waited, though not with complete patience, to hear what the Quaker would say. The man had been matching wits with the devil for some time and, for all his gentleness, was winning, Jip suspected, as often as not.

"My choice," Luke said, "would be to convey thee northward tonight. The rain is on our side. But," he smiled ruefully in the firelight, "it is not mine to choose. If thee and Friend Nelson are to travel together, we must wait until he is more able to make the journey." He stirred the fire and watched it blaze up before continuing. "The enemy will send word to their spies to watch the suspicious houses in this area. I cannot risk conveyance to a station too near at hand. When they companion can make the journey, I aim to convey you to the railroad at Northfield. There is an agent there who is not loath to conceal our passengers in amongst the freight and deliver them safely across the border."

"A real railway?" Jip asked. He'd never seen a train, but the old men at the farm told tales of them—huge black monsters, puffing fire and brimstone as they screamed down their tracks faster than a prize team of Morgans. How would it be to climb into the belly of such a beast and ride? A thrill went down him all the way to his toes. "An *iron* railway?" he asked again to be sure.

"Yes. Not our poor wagon-and-foot underground route. Thee may ride to Canada in style—if we can get there on the day our friend is on duty." Jip determined not to be afraid. A real railway meant Put could *ride* to Canada. Inside where it was warm and dry. They had only to get down the mountain to Northfield.

He bade good night to Luke and mounted the ladder, still shivering at the thought of the great iron beast that would bear him and Put away to Canada and freedom.

He was already awake and hungry again when the first light of early morning penetrated the dark of the cabin. A fellow could get used to good food with hardly any practice. But his breakfast did not appear. By midmorning, tired of lying on the straw mattress listening to the growls from his belly, he climbed down the ladder and stole over to the biscuit crock. He stuffed his pockets. Keeping one eye on the front window, he poured himself a cup of water and carried it and the hardtack back to the loft.

What followed was the longest day of his life. Even at high noon, the cabin let in very little light, so he sat cross-legged on the mattress, tensed for any sound of Luke at the back window. He could hear the birds outside chittering away. He could hear the rustle of leaves, the clatter of squirrels across the wooden shingles over his head. He even thought he heard the squeaking of mice below him. But there was no sound of footsteps on the path or the raising of a window. Luke had promised to come. Something had happened to make him break that vow. What?

His restless brain skittered back and forth across all the possibilities and from there to all the craziness of the last two days, until finally it lit at last on what had been revealed to him: He was an African slave. Not the child of gypsies much less a victim of such. He was the child of a slave—a colored woman had given birth to him. He looked at his hand. In the gloom of the cabin it shone white—far nearer the wool of a merino than the feather of a raven. But then, what did a black African really look like? He had never seen one. There had been a poster hung in Peck's store advertising an abolitionist meeting. The African on the poster did not seem inordinately dark-skinned, though it was hard to tell. At any rate Jip didn't look like that man. And he certainly didn't look like the outlandish caricatures of Negroes in Mr. Lyman's newspaper. But posters and cartoons didn't really tell him what an African slave looked like in the flesh.

Was he shocked to find that he himself was called one? Somewhat, if he were honest. He'd never entertained the possibility before. Of course he was surprised. But the shock that sent quakelike tremors through him was not that he was African, but that he was not entirely Negro. The greater, far more violent assault on his sense of himself was to see his features mirrored in the face of the pale stranger. The very thought made him want to retch. There could be no doubt that his pursuer, the man set to hunt him down like a varmint, was the one who had sired him.

Hour after hour, his poor mind, already pulled about between his anxiety for Put and worry about Luke's not coming, was flooded with revulsion about this new certainty. At first, when Luke had broken the news of his ancestry, he had been numbed. But there in the loft the terribleness of the truth had pierced through that protective wall, leaving him naked to the pain and shame of the fact of his birth.

All those years when he had wondered why no one had bothered to come back for him . . . God must like bitter jokes. Because someone did come. His question was answered. There was no more mystery to be solved. Someone had come back—not to claim his child but to recover his property. He began to shiver though the loft was warm and airless.

Dark came, and still no one appeared to tell him the state of things at the house down the road. A dozen times, he started for the ladder, thinking how he could creep down there himself and scout out how things stood, but he was able to stop himself from such a fool action. If it were possible, Luke Stevens would have come. He had not come. It could only mean that he must wait.

He waited wakeful as an owl. He nibbled up his supply of hardtack, too tense even to lie down for more than a minute or so at a stretch. Then, sometime past midnight, as he judged it, he saw the lights—bobbing high as though borne by men on horseback.

He did not wait for them to arrive. He shoved the cup into his pocket, scrambled down the ladder, and let himself out through the back window as fast as he could. Once he had dropped to the ground, he stood still, listening. Three, no, four horses, coming at a walk up the road. They could only be his pursuers. Luke Stevens would not have come in company and not likely on horseback, even alone.

He crept from the back of the cabin to the edge of the woods. He could hear them dismount, pause, speak quietly at the blocked doorway, and start around the cabin. He did not stop any longer. It was dark in the woods, but he went ahead. If he could get to the stream, he would be able to find their maple tree. Luke might look for him there. And if he did not? What was he to do then? Try to find the way north on his own with no money, no notion of the way, leaving Put behind? Or try to wait his pursuers out? Surely they would tire of hunting him—one half-grown boy, never taught how to be a slave, who'd turn into more of a troublemaker than an asset.

He'd be like the slave George in Teacher's book, he thought. Yes, if caught, he fancied that he'd be quite as belligerent as George toward captivity. Nor would they break him. But slaves like George just got sold down the river to the cotton fields, where they were forced into submission or, like noble Uncle Tom, beaten to an early death.

By the time he stumbled upon the stream the bravado had drained out from the soles of his feet. He did not want to be captured. He did not want his will tested. Oh yes, he could think brave things about freedom being life, but he did not want to have to choose between them. He wanted both.

Must I then jest forget about Put? Leave him with the Stevenses? Who on earth will treat him more kindly than they? Anyone with half a mind would envy such a fate. But if I leave him and go on to Canady by myself, I will be full alone. I need him worse than what he needs me. If only I knew where Teacher was. She'd help me. She'd get me and Put both out of here, clever as she is. . . .

How he found the camping place, he wasn't sure. But there in the pale moonlight through the trees he recognized their tree and flung himself on the wet leaves at its trunk. Did he sleep? He would have said not, but in the first pale gray of morning, something, some noise, startled him wide awake. A crack and crashing through the bush. It was some distance away, but his ear told him whatever it was, man or beast, it was headed in his direction. Should he climb a tree, or wait quietly where he was? It was not likely his pursuers. They would have gone about the chase with more stealth and cunning. No, he reckoned it to be a wild thing of some sort, a bear maybe? He'd heard tales of bears though he had yet to see one.

17

Cries for Help

Through the crash of leaves and litter he heard a voice, a voice weak with exhaustion and desperation: "Jip? Jip, boy, can you hear me?"

Put! He forgot all caution and cried the name aloud. "Put! I'm here. At our old camp. Stay where you are, I'll fetch you." Then he remembered that even trees have ears and he lowered his voice. "Jest keep calling out my name quiet like so's I won't miss you." If the trackers had followed Put into the woods, why, they were both done for, but nothing would keep him from going to Put. When he found him, standing there, his old back bent, his eyes full weary, Jip threw his arms about Put's shoulders and cried like he was Toddy's age—tears of anger and pain, but mostly tears of joy to see his friend again.

Jip led him back across the creek. As he did so, he could feel the man's body shivering. He tried to tell himself it was like his own tears, that Put was just trembling from the pleasure of their being together, but by the time they reached the maple tree he could no longer fool himself. Put's forehead was as hot as a cookstove and his body vibrating like a frightened old ewe at shearing.

Jip started to take off his undershirt—his shirt was

now somewhere in the Stevenses' farmhouse—but Put wouldn't hear of it. "'Twouldn't be decent, you setting around half naked. Good earth and seas, boy, preserve a little delicacy afore an old man."

Jip tried to laugh as he eased Put to the damp ground. They sat in silence, listening to the sounds of the creek. He hardly dared ask the questions that needed to be asked.

"I thought to bring food for us," Put began, "but they who was keeping me prisoner set up all night through in the kitchen, so I daren't."

"Keeping you prisoner?" Had the slavers taken over the farmhouse, then?

"They told me I must stay in bed and not make a sound," he said. "They pushed something afore the door to make sure I didn't escape. But," he smiled proudly, "I'm not such an old fool as I can't manage a little drop from a ground-floor window."

"But where were the Stevenses?" Jip asked. "How could the slavers take over the house?"

"The slavers?" he seemed confused. "It was the plagued Quakers what shut me in."

"Oh, Put. They're our friends. They were trying to keep you safe!"

"They wouldn't let me come to you. I told them to tell you to go on, but they didn't do that neither. They wouldn't listen to me. They just told me I must stay in bed and keep still."

"Because you're sick, Put. They were afraid for you. You're burning with fever."

"They wouldn't let me come to you," he said stubbornly. "Even when I told them you needed me. They

157

wouldn't let me come. I said you'd be caught if we didn't move on, and they wouldn't pay me no mind."

There was nothing more to say. The sun rose high. Even in the shadowy woods, the air felt a bit less chill than it had in the night. Still Put shivered, what teeth he had rattling in his mouth.

Jip took his tin cup and carried cupful after cupful for the old man to drink and some to splash upon his hot forehead. As the day wore on, he knew that another night in the woods might likely be the death of the old man. The cold ground must be painful for him even when the sun was shining.

"How's your feet, Put? Think they could carry us back to the village?"

Put looked up, his eyes bright with fever, but he nodded and began to struggle to stand. Jip pulled him upright. "No hurry a-tall. We'll just meander over that way. We can't go into the village until well past dark, but Mrs. Wilkens is there with Lucy and Toddy and the baby. They're sure to take us in." Put tried to smile.

Any tracker with half a mind could have followed their awkward trail, but the way was mostly downhill, and in the daylight Jip felt confident of the direction. At last they stopped. They were at the edge of the woods in someone's sugar bush, for the maples were scarred from years of tapping. A few minutes more and they could see open pasture through the trees and a farmhouse on the hill beyond.

He tried to figure whose homeplace it was. Was it likely to be friend or foe? Once he got his bearings, he realized it was Baby Tucker's family. He had no idea whether they'd consider harboring a fugitive a crime or a good deed. Best not take a chance. And there was a dog, barking unhappily as though tied against its will. No, best not risk asking for help here.

"Let's back up a bit into the woods," Jip whispered. "I'll find us something to set on—this wet ground's like ice." He found a short piece of trunk from a broken birch and rolled it over against a maple. "There," he said. "There's a parlor chair for you."

Put sat down and leaned against the maple's furrowed trunk, sighing deeply. Jip had thought to bring the cup, though there was no stream handy now. Why hadn't he at least taken the time to fill his pockets with hardtack? He could hardly bear to look at Put, who was hugging his arms to his body, trying to hide the shaking.

Jip left as soon as it was night—sooner gone, sooner returned, he figured. The village was not in total darkness. The moon was nearly full and there were lights shining from a few windows. He kept in the shadows behind the buildings and made his way to the seamstress's shop. There were no lamps lit in front or back. He waited, listening for any sound of activity inside, but could hear none. Good. They were all asleep. Jip crept to a window at the back and stretched his nose over the sill to squint through the glass. He studied every hump until he felt sure that next to the window from where he hunched was a bed and that the bump on it at his right was Lucy's head and the smaller one at the other end was Toddy's head.

He reached up and gently rapped the pane with his knuckles. Lucy stirred and turned over. He rapped again.

Slowly she sat up, then leaned toward the window to peer out into the darkness.

"Lucy?"

She gave a little start.

"It's me, Jip."

She pressed her face on the pane until they were nearly nose to nose against the glass. "Jip? What're you doing here?" she mouthed.

"I need help. Put and me both."

She put her fingers to her lips, looked behind her into the room, and then indicated that he should go to the front of the shop.

He hesitated, not wishing to reveal himself on the street side, but she nodded vigorously and slipped out of bed. Jip sidled around to the front, waited in the shadows until the front door eased open a crack, then crept up on the porch and through the slit.

Lucy didn't bother with a greeting. "You're in terrible trouble," she whispered hoarsely. "There's slavers after you."

"I know. That's why I come—"

"Oh, Jip. Ma heard the slavers offer a hundred dollars' reward and she's licking her chops. If she sees you she'll give you up faster than a cow flicks a fly."

"Your ma?" Mrs. Wilkens had been, if not his friend, surely on his side at the farm. "Why would she do that to me?"

"Ma's mad, Jip. She says you tricked us—making out like you was white as us, when all the time—"

"I didn't know," he said. "Truly. How was I to know?" How could Mrs. Wilkens accuse him of deception?

"I know it don't make sense. But there it is. I'm forbid to speak to you ever again, and if I see you I'm to tell her. But I won't," she added quickly. "I'd never tell. Not even my own ma."

Despair hit him like a blow in the gut. There was to be no help for them—not for Put nor him. What was he to do?

"Teacher'll help you," Lucy whispered. "She's boarding up at Deacon Avery's place the summer. Keeping the books and helping out."

If his heart could have sunk further it would have. Avery'd had no love for him when he was a poor farm brat. He was not likely to jump to his aid now he was a fugitive.

"Lucy?" a sleepy voice called out from the rear room. "Lucy?"

"I better go," she said.

Jip reached into his pocket and pulled out his long-saved penny. "Take this to Peck's and buy some penny candy for you and Toddy, hear? Something to remember your old schoolmate by?"

Her hand closed over the money. "I'll never forget you, Jip. You're my only true friend. You be careful."

He slipped out without another word. The door closed quickly behind him.

What was he to tell Put? That those they had believed to be friends could no longer be counted on? How was he different from the boy Mrs. Wilkens had trusted her Lucy to all last winter? She hadn't despised him when he was a waif fallen off a wagon. Now she's set to betray me—like I done her or her children bodily harm, he thought. He wished he could think that Lucy was lying—rather than believe her ma had said such awful things. But he knew the truth of it. In Mrs. Wilkens's sight, he was no longer just Jip but a thing to be despised. His heart was no different, his mind no better or worse. Nothing about who he was or how he looked had altered in the least, but, suddenly, in other people's heads he was a whole different creature.

Put seemed to be dozing. Jip wanted to leave him there to rest, but he couldn't do that. Suppose he woke up tomorrow and I was gone and he had no notion of where I was or what I was up to? He'd think I'd run off. It might be enough to make him go off into one of his spells, and then where would we be? I'll take him far as Avery's sugar shack. At least there he'll be off the damp ground and out of the chill.

"Put," he whispered. "We got to get moving again."

"You talked to the Wilkenses?"

"I talked to Lucy. It ain't—well, it won't do to stay there. Too dangerous."

For a minute he didn't say anything. Jip waited, loath to tell the whole story. Then he heard something like a sob. He leaned close.

"Don't cry, Put. It's going to be all right. I'm going now to see Teacher. She'll think of a way. It's all right."

Put wiped his nose on his hand. "I knew I should never have come. You'll be caught and . . . What an old fool I was to let you . . ."

"Shush. You think I'll let them weasels snatch us, Put? Come on, now. You and me. We're Green Mountain Boys, ain't we, ain't we, ey?"

Jip grasped Put's arm and pulled him to his feet. He decided not to share his fears about Avery. They hadn't been caught yet. Luck was on their side. Good earth and seas, God himself was on their side. He wouldn't let those devils win. Surely he wouldn't.

"You know something funny? We got to go straight acrost the poor farm to get to Avery's. Did I tell you? Teacher's staying there now, keeping his books. Probably running his whole plaguey business. She's smarter'n any man in this county. You know she went to college?" He kept talking to Put, who stumbled along, his arms clutching his chest, not answering. They crossed Tucker's land, giving the house a wide berth. There were three more small farms between Tucker's and the poor farm. He avoided Tucker's house and barn, but walked across the pasture. Put was just too tired and sick for lengthy detours. When they came to the fields belonging to the poor farm, he ached to steal into the house and find them some food, but he couldn't risk it. A ewe opened a sleepy eye as they passed, and then, recognizing him, pushed to her feet and came over to meet him. He stopped long enough to stroke her nose and murmur.

"She knows me even in the dark, Put." It was warm comfort.

Once beyond poor farm land they headed toward Avery's stand of sugar bush. The wretched man had padlocked his sugar shack. Nobody else in the county had a lock on his house, much less his sugar shack. Once again Jip found a fallen log for Put to sit on. "I'll get Teacher and we'll come for you," he promised and prayed God not to make a liar of him.

He was no sooner out of the protection of the trees than he saw the lights—the high bobbing lights, then the sound of horses beating the hard earth of the road. He fell on his face in the meadow grass. The sheep had nibbled it too close to serve as cover, but he lay paralyzed, listening as the dreadful beat of the hooves grew louder and louder.

He lay there helpless, the wiry grass scratching his cheek. Finally, he turned his head to watch the approach of the horsemen. Where had these demons got their unnatural sense? How could they know where he was headed before he knew it himself? He nearly cried aloud in frustration. There was no use struggling to escape. He was only a stupid boy put off a wagon and raised on a poor farm. How was he supposed to outsmart the devil's own?

18

Capture

What a fool he was! There he lay, his light undershirt shining against the dark grass like a blazing signpost for his enemies. Soon it would be morning. He slithered across the grass on his belly. Beyond him the gray stone of the quarried trough gleamed in the moonlight. On the far side there were piles of slag behind which he could take cover. Surely they would search the house and barns first. He might have a chance, then, to make a run for the woods. He scrambled over the low wall of granite waste. Avery had piled it along the edge of the pasture to keep his cattle from wandering over into the quarry area, where they would soil the surface of the granite or, worse, break a leg on the guttered rock.

The sounds of the horses were ever nearer. Avery's dogs set up the alarm. The horsemen had left the main road and were climbing the hill to Avery's farmhouse. Jip knew he could not make it across the rough stone to the slag piles before the horsemen reached the crest of the hill. He ran toward a wagon loaded with large foundation-sized stones that stood at the near edge of the quarry trough. There were more stones on the quarry itself yet to be loaded. He crouched down behind these and waited for his chance.

The horses had stopped a short distance from the house. He could hear the stamping feet and low whinnies of reined-in mounts and strained to hear what was happening. It was nearly dawn. He needed to run back to the woods while he still had some cover of darkness. Though perhaps he should head the other way—south over the mounds of slag piled on the far side of the trough, which spilled down over the hillside. It would be rough climbing the rubble, but his feet were as leathery as old boots after years of barefoot life. If he could get across the open rock of the quarry trough without being spied—

Avery's dogs began to bark more frantically. He had no fear of Avery's dogs. They were his friends from sugaring time. But their frenzied barks must mean that the riders were at the house now. He crept around the edge of the stones. He had to see where they were.

He could make out the shadowed bulk of them grouped near the door of the farmhouse. Perhaps some of them had gone in. Now was his chance. He must get over the slag and down the hill. The first light of morning was already turning the dome of the sky to gray.

Jip left the shelter of the foundation stones and made his way up and down the gutters of the quarry, willing himself invisible. Then he heard the dogs bay. Someone had set them loose. Soon they would find him and betray him.

If he could make it to the slag in time—but it was too late. The three dogs spotted him and set up a hunting chorus, leaping nimbly across the pocked surface of the quarry in his direction.

A cry went up. "There he is!"

He tried to scramble up the slag pile, but the stones

were not fixed. They came tumbling down toward him, hitting his ankles and legs until he stood buried, nearly to the knees. Each time he tried to lift his bruised legs out and climb, the stones shifted and held him fast. By now the dogs had recognized their friend. They jumped about to miss the stones his climbing had dislodged. They were barking with joy to see him, wagging their tails in delight.

"Turn around and come down."

Over his shoulder he could see the slave catcher making his way cautiously across the granite face. His hand was out and at the end of it Jip could make out the shape of a large derringer pistol.

Luke had said that they would not want to injure him, but how could he be sure? It hardly mattered. He could not escape.

"Come down off those rocks. I don't want to have to hurt you," the slaver called out.

Others were coming from the house, the pale man at their lead. "Call off your dogs, Mr. Avery," the pale man ordered as he picked his way across the granite.

"They won't bother him none," Avery said.

"Call off your dogs, sir," the man repeated tightly.

Avery whistled. The dogs gave Jip a sad look and reluctantly returned to their master's side.

"Tie them up."

Avery cocked his head and opened his mouth, but seemed to reconsider. "C'mon, boys," he said and started for his house, his unhappy dogs at his heels.

"You can come down now," the pale man said. "The dogs won't hurt you."

Slowly, taking care not to set the stones tumbling

again, Jip freed first one bruised foot and then the other and then half ran half fell back down the slag to face his captors. They backed up hastily as Jip sent more stones tumbling down the pile.

"Tie his hands behind him," the pale man said, throwing a length of rope to Addison Brackett.

"I was right, wasn't I?" Addison said. "Didn't I say he'd run to Teacher?"

"Just tie him up," the man said again.

"Don't you dare, Addison Brackett." It was Teacher herself, calling out as she came as fast as she could make it across the uneven rock. Her dark hair was bound in one long untidy pigtail, her feet bare. Addison, always terrified by what the pupils called Teacher's look, stepped back.

She turned to the sheriff. "What is the meaning of this, Mr. Glover?" she asked.

Sheriff Glover looked embarrassed. "Wal, miss, the gent does got a warrant."

"From God Almighty?" Her eyes flashed.

The pale man stepped between Teacher and the sheriff. "This is not your affair, madam," he said. "It is a matter of law, nothing to concern a lady."

She opened her mouth and would have said more except that the slave catcher, his pistol still trained on Jip, suddenly interrupted. "What's that?"

In the morning stillness Jip heard it, sweet as a birdcall: a high, clear tenor voice singing Toddy's hymn:

"Is it death, is it death?
That soon will quench, will quench this mortal flame?"

At first Jip thought it must be Put's ghost, letting him know that all was well, that his friend was past all worry now, but he could tell that all the others had heard it, too. And then they saw him coming across the grass, a tall ragged form, his head thrown back as he sang to the sky.

"It's our lunatic," Jip said.

The slaver's hand began to shake. He waved the pistol. "You got to call to him," he said. "Settle him down."

"It ain't no use," Jip said. "When he's raving, can't no one calm him, even me." *God forgive my lying tongue.*

"But he's coming this way."

"He's kinda like my dog. Even when he's craziest, he don't like it if someone messes with me."

> "There's not a cloud that doth arise,
> To hide my Jesus from my eyes.
> I soon shall mount the upper skies . . ."

Still singing, the old man threw one leg over the slag wall and then the other. He kept coming, past the wagon, past the pile of stone, right toward the crowd of them gathered there on the quarry floor. Friend and enemy alike watched as though in a trance as the lunatic started across the bedrock, not bothering to watch his footing, just keeping his eyes on the slave catcher.

"I don't like it," the slave catcher said. He was trembling all over. "I don't like lunatics."

"Quiet, fool," the pale man said.

"You ain't scairt, are you, mister?" Jip asked.

As if to answer, the slave catcher turned the pistol away from Jip and pointed it toward the old man. "Stop! Stop right there!" Put kept walking.

Oh, dear God. *He thinks he can save me.* "Don't, Put!" Jip yelled out. "Go back!"

" 'Tune, tune your harps, your harps ye saints on high . . .' " He was singing at the top of his voice: " 'I too will strike my harp . . .' " He was nearly upon the slave catcher now.

A shot rang out. Put stopped, a look of utter surprise on his face, then with a shout, " 'All is well!' " he threw his body forward. As though propelled by some supernatural strength, he hurled himself upon the slaver as the man tried desperately to reload. With his clawlike hands, Put grabbed the slaver's arms and drove him back furiously against the piled foundation stones.

His top hat fell off. Then the man's skull struck a jagged edge of granite with a crack like that of a pumpkin bursting. The pistol flew high into the air, bounced once against the quarry floor and lay still. Like partners in some horrible dance, Put and the slaver crumpled, sliding slowly to the bedrock, still locked in their cursed embrace.

Oh, Put, no. Jip started toward his friend, but a hand grabbed his arm.

"Lemme go!" he cried out. "I got to see to him!"

"He's dead." The voice was as tight as the grip on his arm.

"No, no, not my Put." He turned to look at his captor. "Kill me," he sobbed. "Kill me, but don't kill my Put. He ain't done nothing to you. Please, please don't hurt him."

The gray eyes stared into his. There was a flicker of something near kin to shame in them. A shudder went through the man's body as he turned away. "You, boy," he called out to Addison. "I said, tie him up." Without looking at Jip again, he let go of his arm and went over

170

to where Sheriff Glover and Teacher bent over the fallen men.

Jip knew Put was dead. Of course he knew, but, until Teacher came back to where the Bracketts guarded him, and he could see the deep sorrow in her eyes, he had tried to hope.

Avery was coming back across the quarry from his house. The pale man picked up the derringer and, calling out, ordered him to see to the bodies.

"What were you planning to do with the boy?" Teacher asked.

The pale man took a watch out of his pocket as though to check the time. "I'm taking the fugitive back to where he belongs," he said.

"Not until after the hearing, you won't."

"Now listen here, young woman . . ."

"Tell him, Mr. Glover."

Sheriff Glover shifted his gaze uneasily from one to the other. It was plain that he didn't know what Teacher meant.

"Habeas corpus, Mr. Glover. Explain that the boy is entitled to a hearing in a court of law."

"Ridiculous. This is my property."

Sheriff Glover took one last look at Teacher before clearing his throat to reply. "Wal, now, come to think of it, mister, I think the lady's got a point. You may know the boy belongs to you. And for all I know the boy knows that. It's jest that the law don't know that—" He spat on the granite. "Yit."

"You know you are bound by the Fugitive Slave Act to give me every assistance—"

"Yah, wal, up here in Vermont folks think you got to prove this here boy's your legal property afore you can haul him acrost the line into Massachusetts, where I hear tell there's some what ain't quite so particular."

The pale man grew whiter still. He looked about. But he stood alone. Even the Bracketts hesitated to cross both Teacher and the law.

"No need to fret, mister," the sheriff continued. "He's jest a ignorant boy raised on our town poor farm. He can hardly best you—a gentleman of your stripe. Meantime, I'll jest hold him in the jail for you."

The Brackett brothers boosted Jip up on the deputy's horse, never daring to look the boy in the eye. And Jip, hands bound, head sagging in despair against his chest, rode into the village behind the deputy, leaving Put stretched out on the bedrock of the quarry, his eyes still wide open in surprise.

19

End and Beginning

What the sheriff had rather grandly referred to as "the jail" was only a small room in the basement of the town hall where the village put public drunks or the occasional vagrant for safekeeping. There were no bars on the one small high window, as no one had ever tried to escape. The cell door was a simple wooden one with a bolt on the outside to keep an unruly inmate from roaming the building during the night.

The pale man spotted the careless security measures at once and paid the deputy from his own pocket to spend the nights in the corridor outside the room until the hearing.

He needn't worry, Jip thought, I ain't going nowhere. He sat on the edge of the wooden cot. The room smelled of the tramps and drunkards who'd been there before him and was none too clean, but he hardly noticed.

Luke Stevens tried to warn me. He tried to tell me not to take Put with me, but I was too proud, too ornery to heed him. Pigheaded fool. Caring more for myself than for Put. I was wrong. The slavers didn't kill him. I did.

The only punishment that nearly fit his monstrous crime was bondage. To go meekly with that pale devil and live out the rest of his miserable life in whatever hell that one chose to confine him to.

The hearing was set for two days hence. Sheriff Glover had explained to the pale man that the prisoner must have a day to make ready his defense, and since the day following was a Sabbath, the judge would not be available until Monday. Jip did not plan any defense, and it was irksome to him to have his sentence so delayed.

He had been in jail for several hours when the door opened and the sheriff told him he had visitors. Teacher had come, Luke Stevens with her. They brought him his overshirt, now washed and mended, and a basket of food.

"I was to bring you food yesterday," Luke said apologetically, handing him the neatly packed basket, "but the slavers seemed to have eyes everywhere. How thy friend escaped their notice, God help me, I'll never know—"

"I ain't hungry," Jip said. "Begging your pardon."

"No," said Teacher, sitting down on the cot beside him, "probably not. But try to take something. You need your strength."

"What—what of Put?" he asked.

"We fetched him back," Luke's voice faltered, "back up to our house, my brothers and I."

"He ought to have—I want him to have a proper funeral."

Teacher put her hand gently on Jip's. "I promise you. In the church."

"With hymns?"

She nodded. "With hymns."

"There's one he's partial to." Jip couldn't quite bring himself to say it was the one Put died singing. "Lucy will know the one."

He began to cry then. He had thought he was past all feeling, but when he thought of the hymn, the picture of Put coming across the pasture, his head thrown back . . . "Do you think—I mean, is it—all well with him now?"

"Yes," she said. "I'm sure."

He wiped his eyes on the back of his hand. Teacher handed him a handkerchief. Her own eyes were bright with tears. "We have to think of you now, Jip."

He shook his head.

"What does thee mean?" Luke Stevens bent his head close to Jip's and whispered hoarsely. "Surely thee is not resigned to slavery?"

Jip couldn't meet the Quaker's gaze, for that was exactly what he had determined.

"Then," Teacher's eyes flashed as though he were an insolent student, "then you mean to throw poor Put's life away?"

"No." He looked at her horrified. How could she imagine—

"He died for you, Jip. And you mean to make that of no account?" She was whispering so no one outside in the corridor could hear, but the whisper only served to make her fury more apparent. She stood up and began to pace the small room.

Now Luke came close to the cot. "I mean to spirit thee away," he said in Jip's ear. "We have a friend in Montreal—Ezekial Freeman. We will get thee there. Very early Monday morning the train will stop in North-field. Tomorrow night . . ."

"No," Jip said between his teeth. "They'd punish you sure—for aiding a runaway."

"I've been at this game for many a year now . . ."

"Wait." Teacher had stopped her pacing. "No one needs to spirit anyone away. We just need to put on a defense—one that will convince the justice." She smiled. "The man has no love for slavers. He'll not be hard to convince."

"There ain't no defense," Jip said dully. "You know the devil speaks the truth."

"Ah, Jip, boy, he's only a man. A poor sinner like me or thee."

Teacher spun around. "The devil never speaks the truth!"

Jip couldn't tell which of them she was rebuking. She didn't explain, only went on in the same manner in which she'd give out the solution to a problem in arithmetic: "You have never known it, Jip, but you are my son."

"Marm?"

She blew out a sigh and sat down beside him on the cot. "I was indiscreet those years ago when I was a factory girl in Lowell. It happened among us mill girls more often than—"

Teacher was lying! He'd never imagined such a thing. A woman so noble lying like some scoundrel. "It ain't true. You know it ain't true. Why do you say such a monstrous thing about yourself?"

She looked him in the eye. "I'm ready to swear to it before the justice," she said. "I want to acknowledge that you are my child."

Jip turned to Luke. "You won't let her do such a thing, will you? Lying and breaking the law? Bringing disgrace on herself?"

Luke smiled wryly. "The woman has her own mind. If

she's made it up, it's not likely she'll suddenly start listening to me."

"I thought you cared about her!" He said it right out loud.

Now Luke was looking Teacher full in the face. "She knows I do. Surely she does." He walked over to Teacher, took her hands, and pulled her gently to her feet. "If thee is determined on such a headstrong and desperate course, I cannot stop thee. But I will say on Monday that I am the father of the boy. Before the justice I will plead for forgiveness and beg thee to be my wife."

"They'll dismiss you from the Meeting," she said to him, leaving her hands in his.

"They'll dismiss me for marrying anyone who is outside the Meeting," he said, with a little laugh, "even when the Meeting is without young women to marry."

"Then you are determined to do this foolish thing?"

"Since the day thee walked down the hill to sell thy heifer to my father," he said.

"For a Quaker, you are an uncommonly stubborn man."

"And thee, Lyddie Worthen, are the world's most stubborn woman. Are we not a proper pair?"

They said more, but Jip had given up listening. His ears would not let him be party to such a wicked conspiracy. Luke's being cast out of the Quaker Meeting was nothing compared to what folks would say of her.

He waited well past dark, until he could hear the deputy's snoring through the door. The man had been awake all the previous night tracking Jip down, so Jip had reason to hope that his sleep would be deep.

He put the buns and slabs of cheese that his visitors had brought into his shirtfront and tied his shirttails tightly together to keep the food safe. Then he inched the cot over to the window and, covering the food basket with the quilt from the cot, swung it against the glass. There was hardly any sound, but he waited, hardly breathing, to make sure he hadn't waked the deputy.

The snoring seemed as regular as before. By standing on the cot, Jip could just touch the window with his fingertips. He brushed the glass off the frame with the end of the quilt and then pulled himself up to the broad sill. It was easy then, to slide across it onto the ground outside.

He came out into a clear August night. Follow the North Star. Put had showed him the way. Jip looked up at the heavens to get his bearing from the Big Dipper and then began to run.

I found the Reverend Ezekial Freeman in Montreal with very little trouble. Teacher and Luke's friend was the only African minister called by that name in the city. The Freemans have given me the family and the name I was long denied. They have brought me up to be a Freeman among free peoples. I am very grateful. I doubt that I could have learned the art of living as a man both black and free without their compassionate instruction.

But my heart still yearns for the land I left behind. My old country is at war. A Negro regiment is forming in New York, and I have decided to go south and join the struggle. My foster mother weeps to see me go, but my foster father understands even though he is a clergyman and a man of gentle spirit.

It is the opposite with my friends at home. Luke Stevens does not countenance war and begs me to remain here, while his wife, my dear Teacher, sends me her blessing. (It seems that the excuse of my defense was not needed to push the two of them into marriage after all.) Teacher declares that were she not a woman and a mother, she would be at my side, rifle in hand.

But who can say which of us is right in this wretched business? Surely the Almighty, who would not have us enslave one another, does not rejoice to see us kill each other in His name.

Yet, I will return now to do what it seems I must. As I

go, I try to cling to the faith that Put used to sing—to believe that all is well, whether I live a free man or die to secure that freedom for others. Nonetheless, had I a choice, I would choose a little plot of rocky land in the Green Mountains with a flock of sheep and a peaceful old age.

ALL IS WELL

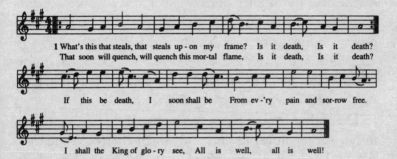

1 What's this that steals, that steals up-on my frame? Is it death, Is it death?
That soon will quench, will quench this mor-tal flame, Is it death, Is it death?

If this be death, I soon shall be From ev-'ry pain and sor-row free.

I shall the King of glo-ry see, All is well, all is well!

2 Weep not, my friends, my friends weep not for me, All is well, all is well!
My sins forgiv'n, forgiv'n and I am free, All is well, all is well!
There's not a cloud that doth arise, To hide my Jesus from my eyes.
I soon shall mount the upper skies, All is well, all is well!

3 Tune, tune your harps ye saints on high, All is well, all is well!
I too will strike my harp with equal joy, All is well, all is well!
Bright angels are from glory come, They're round my bed, they're in my room,
They wait to waft my spirit home, All is well, all is well!

4 Hark! hark! my Lord, my Lord and Master's voice, Calls away, calls away!
I soon shall see—enjoy my happy choice, Why delay, why delay?
Farewell, my friends, adieu, adieu, I can no longer stay with you,
My glittering crown appears in view, All is well, all is well!

5 Hail, hail! all hail, all hail! ye blood-washed throng, Saved by grace, saved by grace!
I come to join, to join your rapturous song, Saved by grace, saved by grace,
All, all is peace and joy divine, And heaven and glory now are mine,
Loud hallelujahs to the Lamb, All is well, all is well!

Words and music Anonymous

Katherine Paterson's books have received wide acclaim and been published in twenty languages. Among her many literary honors are two Newbery Medals, for *Bridge to Terabithia* and *Jacob Have I Loved*, two National Book Awards, and most recently the Hans Christian Andersen Award. Her latest book is *Parzival*.

The author lives in Barre, Vermont, an area she describes in her earlier novel *Lyddie*, and which she researched for the background of this story. The Patersons have four grown children and two grandchildren.

More information about Katherine Paterson is available at her website, Terabithia (**http://www.terabithia.com**).